Bradley H. Pierce

ISBN: 978-0-9913660-0-2 (Print Version)

Printed in the U.S.A.

January 2014 Edition

In Memory
of
Laura Denese Humphries

CONTENTS

PRELUDE

Several years ago, I began a journey to help the homeless of my community. This endeavor led to the formation of an outreach called The Bridge Ministry. The focus of this ministry became a group of men and women who lived under a bridge at the edge of my town. Each week, I would visit the bridge, taking them food and items that they could use. Over time, lines of communication opened, and then relationships began to form. Eventually, these relationships turned into real friendships. Through the telling of their stories, they offered me intimate, personal glimpses into their lives. In the process, I started seeing some parallels between my life and theirs. Gradually, I began to see myself in them, because their stories had some similarities with my own. For a man who had never known a true day of hardship, this was a real eye opener. From these encounters, I was pressed to look long and hard into what had become, in effect, a mirror, seeing myself as I never had before. What followed was a time of deep reflection into the purpose and meaning of my life.

The following story was born during this period of time. It began as a fictional tale, an allegory of sorts, about my life and ministry at the bridge. But God had different plans for my book. Somewhere along the way, my story evolved into more than a simple tale about one man's journey to self-discovery. Into the very fabric of my story, God wove another tale, and the substance of this second storyline became a homeless woman named Denese. She lived under the bridge, and she was my first project, so to speak. I had great hopes that I could help her get better. So, as I wrote her character into my fictional story, I envisioned a happy ending for her, one in which God redeemed her life. However, like my fictional story, her true story also evolved during the writing of this book. It deviated from the path that I had intended. I planned a happy ending for her, but in real life, this was not the case. Her life ended in a bitter-sweet fashion, and the only reason that it was sweet at all was because God did eventually redeem her life but not in the way that I imagined. I had always hoped and prayed for a real-life miracle to occur in her life while she was living. But, in a curious twist, her miracle didn't come until much later. The second part of this book is dedicated to how this miracle came into being. It is a non-fictional narrative that was written several years after the first story had been completed.

Yours truly,
Brad Pierce

PART ONE

ONE

It had been an unseasonably cold and wet winter for the inhabitants of Happyville. The rain had been coming down almost continuously for a year. Some days it would drizzle. Other days it might come down in buckets, and on a few days, the rain dropped out of the sky in the form of frozen pellets. The lakes and rivers were filled to the brim, and on a few occasions, after a particularly heavy rain, they overflowed into some of the neighboring homes and businesses of Happyville. The ground was thoroughly soaked and had become more like a bog than dry land. Underfoot, it felt soggy and squishy to walk upon, and as such, it had become completely unsuitable for playing. As a result, both child and adult had been confined indoors. During the days, they went to school or work, and at night they huddled idly within their homes.

The days had become quite boring, and the atmosphere in Happyville had become anything but happy. In fact, it had become downright morose, but the social and recreational climate of Happyville wasn't all that the rain had affected. It had permeated into the economics of the town as well, for Happyville was a place where people came to be just that...happy. On a normal day, the town would be a bustle of activity as people from the far corners of Happy Land came to spend their time, and more importantly, their money, while they enjoyed its amusement parks, zoos, and many other forms of recreation. But the rain had all but halted the commerce within Happyville because each business was extensively interwoven with the next, and no people meant no business for anyone. Thus, the inhabitants of Happyville were sad not just because they had been cooped up inside for many months but because their very livelihoods had been threatened.

With shrinking bank accounts, the people of Happyville stopped spending money on activities that carried the sole purpose of pleasure. This forced them to spend time at home with their friends and families. Soon they realized that they didn't know how to interact with each other, or with themselves for that matter, and when they did, they weren't sure if they really even liked one another. What they discovered was that for far too long they had been masquerading behind a cloud of busyness, believing that by virtue of staying busy they would be happy. Some busied themselves with the accumulation of money and possessions. Others busied themselves with activities of all sorts. In fact, there was a busyness that could be ascribed to anything imaginable under the sun, and most if not all of the inhabitants of Happy Land had become quite adept in perfecting the art of busyness. Despite their noblest efforts, their busyness failed to live up to their expectations, and in the end, it only left them feeling tired, burned out, and empty. And in one of the greatest ironies of all time, the people of Happyville realized that they had been living a lie and that they were truly anything but happy.

Compounding their dilemma was the fact that they did not know how to fix themselves, or in simpler terms, they were at a loss as to how to attain real happiness. They had only been doing what they had been taught, which is exactly what their parents before them had been taught to do. To break from this pattern would be to deviate into the unknown, and for most, the pain of staying in their current predicament was more bearable than the fear and anxiety that would result by stepping outside of their comfort zones. So, they remained in the vicious cycle in which they found themselves. As the rain continued, they discovered that they had less and less to do, which meant that they also had less and less busyness to medicate away their blues. The end result was that the whole town had begun to slip away into a deep and dark depression.

And so our tale begins in a small home on the northern outskirts of Happyville, the capital and northernmost town of Happy Land. It was a modest home by all accounts. It had two bedrooms, one bath, and a small kitchen that was connected to a similarly sized den. It didn't have all of the amenities of some of the larger homes closer to town, but it was all that the Buerger family of three could afford. Mr. Buerger was a maintenance man at Happy World, the largest amusement park in Happyville, and due to the drop in attendance, he had been all but laid off. Mrs. Buerger was a waitress at Cup of Fun coffee shop, and for months she had barely made enough to justify her daily drive to work. To say that money was tight would be an understatement. With each new day, it became exceedingly more difficult for them to keep their heads above water, both literally and figuratively, and the constant pressure had begun to put a tremendous strain on the dynamics within the home.

Like most fathers and husbands, Mr. Buerger felt that it was his duty to provide for his family like his father before him had done, and when he couldn't, it began to eat away at him like a worm gnaws a hole in an apple. Then one day, he turned to alcohol in hopes of finding a little solace and comfort for the shame and guilt that he felt, and in a bottle of Jim Beam, Mr. Buerger found something that would at least numb his pain for a little while. Then like all good Happyvillians, he began busying himself with the task of emptying his bottle of Jim Beam every day. At first, Mrs. Buerger protested, but as the days turned into weeks, her protesting turned into complaining, and as the weeks turned into months, her complaining turned into crying. To Brad, the Buerger's only child, it seemed as if her tears were as constant as the raindrops that fell from the sky. But Mrs.

Buerger's tears weren't simply because her husband had become an alcoholic; they flowed most intensely because he had become a quite an abusive one, and it was to the misery of Mr. Buerger's twelve-year-old son, Brad, that most of his abuse had been targeted toward him. Initially, the abuse was only verbal, but as Mr. Buerger's soul began to harden, the abuse became physical. Over time, Mr. Buerger's abuse of his son grew more violent and more frequent, and it wasn't all that unusual for Brad to miss two or three days of school each week while he mended from some of his father's more vicious attacks.

On the day that our story began, Mr. Buerger was in a particularly foul mood, and he had decided to take out his anger on his son once more. The verbal taunts quickly escalated to slaps in the face, and when Mr. Buerger had become bored of this activity, he decided to try something new. He went over to the fireplace and picked up the poker. He had left it sitting by the fire with its tip buried in the coals. The pointy tip glowed a fiery, orange color. Brad cowered in the corner, paralyzed with fear. But as his father neared him carrying the hot poker, the primitive part of Brad's brain took control, and it triggered the instinct of survival. Following it, he fled in a direction opposite his father and quickly escaped through the front door. Once outside, he was met by a hard, down-pouring rain. Visibility was poor, but rather than turn back, he proceeded forward into the watery abyss. His father followed behind him but in short order slipped and fell into the mud. Without hesitation, Brad continued to move as fast as his legs could carry him, leaving behind his father and the hateful accusations he was shouting.

For a very long time Brad continued running, following an abandoned road that led north of town. He had taken walks on this road before, but he had never gone as far as he had on this day. With no desire to turn back, he continued to follow the old road. He had no plan. He simply wanted to get very far away from his father. While he ran, his mind was in a continual state of motion, and it brought to the forefront thoughts and emotions that he normally tried to forget. Feelings of anger, sadness, confusion, and inadequacy began to spring from within. Most days, he was successful at keeping these feelings repressed. It was his method of coping with all that was so wrong in his world, and it was through this coping mechanism that he was able to survive from day to day. But, on this particular afternoon, his feelings refused to be suppressed, and they began pouring out.

As he ran, Brad began boxing and kicking against the air, stomping in mud puddles, and screaming at the top of his voice. The flurry of activity and outburst of emotion quickly exhausted him. His running slowed to a mere walk. It was at this point that he realized that he was soaked to the bone, and with every passing moment, the heat that had been generated from his running began to dissipate—his body began growing colder and colder. With folded arms, he hunched over and continued against the driving rain, but as he walked, the enormity of his situation started pressing down on him, and just like the heat that had dissipated from his body, any remaining hope in his heart began to dissipate as well. In this moment, his current plight was shown for what it really was. He was helplessly alone, and not just in the sense that he was standing in the middle of nowhere. He felt alone in a much larger sense. All that he wanted was to be held, to be understood, to be loved. But the truth is that he felt very unloved, and he knew of no one who could give him what he needed. Then he experienced something that no twelve-year-old should ever have to experience.

Overwhelmed with grief, Brad's spirit suddenly broke, and when it did, he collapsed onto his knees and started sobbing uncontrollably into his hands. In the midst of his crying, he pondered very valid questions like "Why was I born?" and "What is the purpose of living?" Eventually, this sadness thoroughly pervaded him and brought him to a place where he was lying face down in the mud. He wished that the rain would drown him and end his misery. With the passage of time, however, it became apparent that this wish would not come true. In fact, quite the opposite happened. The rain began to slow from a downpour to a gentle drizzle. Initially, Brad hoped that this might be a sign that better things were yet to come, but what he quickly realized as he surveyed the scene was that the slowing of the rain had only served to help him see the real sign. It was an actual sign, one that read "Dead End–Bridge Closed." Even at the tender age of twelve, Brad could see the sad irony of this sign—his sign. Then, mustering what strength he had left, he gathered himself, stood up, and began walking toward what he believed would be his actual dead end.

With his head hanging low, Brad slowly made his way up the hill. Once at the top, he stopped dead in his tracks. The scene was simply breathtaking. He imagined that a painter would be hard pressed to capture the full beauty of what his eyes beheld because stretched out before him was a long valley with a large river flowing through it. From one side of the river to the other, the distance must have been one mile in length. It was impossible to estimate the river's depth as the water was the color of chocolate, but he surmised that it was probably just as deep as it was wide. Ahead, the road led to a wooden bridge, which was in shambles. The middle third of the bridge was completely missing, and the parts that were still standing looked as if they would soon join the mid-section of the bridge at the bottom of the river. As Brad watched the river batter against the old, broken bridge, tears began flowing down his face again. The image moved him, for it reminded him in many ways of himself. In particular, he felt a strong connection to the bridge, for like the bridge, he had been battered until there was little left but the decaying remains of who and what he had once been.

He slowly made his way toward the bridge. Once there, he paused before proceeding any further. From his place atop the hill, the bridge had seemed relatively small, but from his new vantage point, his perspective about the bridge had changed. As he stood next to it, he realized that he was actually the one who was relatively small because the bridge, although old and dilapidated, was massive in both size and scope. Huge timbers had been sunk into the riverbed, and they formed the base upon which the remainder of the bridge had been built. Over the sunken timbers, long, thick wooden planks had been laid, and they served as the floor of the bridge. The lattice high above had been constructed in such a manner that the roof appeared to be supported by thousands of large crosses. As he stared down the seemingly endless corridor, he wondered how old the bridge was, who built it, what was on the other side, and finally why had it been so neglected.

From these thoughts, his mind inevitably drifted back to his own predicament and the pain that it was causing. He decided that he no longer wanted to bear the burden of this pain and that death would be preferable to continuing life in this way. To end his suffering, his plan was to throw himself from the bridge into the chilly waters that raged just below. To end his life by drowning seemed rather fitting since his misery had begun over a year ago with the arrival of the rain. As he stepped onto the bridge and began walking toward the missing section, the image of the sign that read "Dead End–Bridge Closed" flashed into his mind. Tears welled up in his eyes again. Emotionally and physically, he was drained and on the verge of breaking down when something caught his attention. It was a sound that could faintly be heard over the rain and river. It was the sound of someone or something crying. With his curiosity heightened, he stopped and strained his ears to listen. Quickly, he detected that the source of the crying was coming from underneath the bridge. Not knowing exactly what he should do, he decided to remain still and simply listen. Strangely enough, he felt some comfort in knowing that someone or something felt as sorrowful as he did, and in this moment, he felt a connection that tugged on his heartstrings. In fact, he had almost convinced himself that he should forgo his own ill-fated plans and instead go to this creature's aid. But then something happened. A different noise, quite unlike the first, began to resonate from directly underneath him. It was the sound of cracking and popping, and before Brad realized what was happening, he felt the bridge underneath him give way. He lost his balance and fell backwards through the floor as it collapsed. On the way down, his head smacked firmly against one of the bridge's undergirders. The force from the blow knocked him completely out. After he lost consciousness, Brad's body no longer fought. It plunged lifelessly into the chilly waters below, and once caught in the current, it quickly disappeared downstream.

TWO

Two weeks later, Brad awoke. Much to his surprise, he realized that he was not at home but in the Happyville hospital. Once the excitement over his miraculous improvement had waned, he learned the facts about his hospitalization. During his stay, he had remained unconscious, lying in a deep coma. The doctors felt that his coma had resulted from some type of head injury. To further complicate matters, he had developed a case of double pneumonia shortly after arriving. Once he had survived the first week, the doctors increased his chance of survival to fifty percent. However, they were still very concerned about his recovery in the event that he did survive, and they warned the family that he would probably suffer from some form of permanent brain injury. When he was found to be completely normal, there was much room for celebration because not only had he returned, but he had returned whole, at least on the surface. Deep down, he still held the pain, and those wounds had not healed. While the doctors and hospital staff around him smiled and cried tears of joy, he was left to sadly ponder his not-so-distant past and the uncertainty of his future.

While Brad was in his coma, an interesting development had occurred at home. News of Brad's illness had spread throughout Happyville, and one individual in particular had developed a rather keen interest in his case. This individual happened to be the local sheriff. He had heard the rumors about

Mr. Buerger's alcoholic binges and the volatile behavior that had resulted from them. After conducting an investigation into his case, the sheriff concluded that Mr. Buerger had attempted to kill his son. Mr. Buerger adamantly denied these allegations, but all those involved in his case suspected that he was just too drunk to remember. Thus, Mr. Buerger was not there to greet his son when he awoke, nor was he there to greet him when he came home, because he was in jail serving a 23-year sentence for attempted murder. The specifics about Mr. Buerger's absence were concealed from Brad, feeling it was in his best interests. So he was left to form his own conclusion that his father was in prison because he was an alcoholic and a child abuser but never because he was an attempted murderer.

With his father out of the picture, Brad's life changed a great deal. His mother was gone much of the day, waitressing at the Cup of Fun coffee shop. Her usual routine was to leave early and come home late. On rare occasions, she might cook, but she usually brought home leftovers from the restaurant. Most nights, she would just leave them on the table, and then without uttering a single word, she would retreat to her bedroom where she would cry herself to sleep. In the mornings, Brad would dress for school and eat whatever was left from the previous night. School wasn't much better. He had been an introvert all of his life so making friends had always proven difficult, but after his return, it had become even more so. For the most part the children, as well as the teachers, acted as though he wasn't there. He ate lunch alone. He played alone. Rarely was a word ever spoken to him. This is how Brad's life changed after his father was gone. He went from being the center of one man's brutality to essentially being non-existent to an entire community. He had left one hell only to enter another.

* * * *

One evening, Brad was rummaging through a pile of books and papers in the den in an attempt to find something with which to occupy himself. While searching, he happened upon a copy of the *Happyville Bridge*, a local newsletter about the town. As he studied the emblem of the bridge, his mind returned to that fateful day when he found the old wooden bridge north of town. He had not thought much of that day or any other for that matter, but the picture of the bridge had rekindled some forgotten memories as well as some unanswered questions. Toting the copy of the magazine, he went to his mother's bedroom and knocked on the door. She composed herself as best she could and then responded to his knocking by saying, "Come in." Brad slowly opened the door to find his mother lying on the bed amidst a sea of used tissues.

He approached cautiously, and when he felt that it was safe to proceed he asked, "Mother, who rescued me from the river?"

His mother shot him a look of confusion and asked, "What do you mean exactly?"

"You know...the day that I went to the hospital...who saved me from the river?"

At the mere mention of that fateful day, his mother became notably upset. "Don't ever mention that day again! Now get out and leave me alone!" she screamed as she flung the tissue box at him. Brad scurried out of her room, and his mother slammed the door behind him as he left.

* * * *

Later that week, Brad met Mr. Jones, the mailman, at the door, and through casual conversation, he discovered that Mr. Jones had actually been the one who had discovered his nearly lifeless body while delivering the mail. He had found Brad lying unconscious next to the front door and subsequently notified his parents. Obviously, this information came as quite a shock to Brad as he had been wondering who had saved him from the river. Now, he had the additional question of how he got from the river to his house. To unravel this mystery, Brad figured that he would have to return to the bridge.

On Friday night, alone as usual in his room, Brad planned his return visit to the bridge, but when it came time for bed, sleep did not come easily as his mind continued to race. Most of his apprehension centered upon the mysterious crying from under the bridge. He wondered who or what would live under a bridge, and more importantly, would this creature be a friend or foe. As he pondered these thoughts, his imagination began to get the better of him, and very quickly he realized that what had been a source of comfort at the time had now become a source of fear. Like most, he feared the unknown, and his imagination only served to feed his fear. By morning, Brad was quite certain that a monster lived under the bridge, and if he went back there, it would gobble him up. Naturally, he convinced himself that it wasn't safe and he shouldn't go. But as the morning hours slowly passed, his curiosity began to mount. Gradually his fears were supplanted by the desire to know what had happened to him on that day.

Around noon, he decided that he was going. Before leaving, he packed a lunch, and at the door, he put on his raincoat because the weather, as usual, was overcast and rainy. Following the old abandoned road, Brad retraced his steps to the bridge. He walked through the large puddles that he had angrily stomped in previously. He passed the old sign that read, "Dead End–Bridge Closed." He paused once again at the top of the hill that overlooked the valley before continuing onward. As he drew closer to the bridge, his heart began to beat wildly in his chest. Terrible visions and thoughts began to fill his mind again. His senses of sight, hearing, and smell were heightened. Somewhat paranoid, his gaze nervously shifted from side to side as he looked for any signs of danger. Meanwhile, his courage began to rapidly fade as he inched ever closer to the bridge. After what seemed like a lifetime, but in reality was only a couple of minutes, he finally made it to the bridge.

All in all, Brad found that the bridge was relatively unchanged except for one notable exception. The floor that previously had been intact had a huge, gaping hole torn into it. Once again, he felt a strong connection to the bridge, because like the bridge, he had a large empty place in his heart, and he knew that, just like the bridge, if no one ever fixed that empty place then it would remain empty forever. After much deliberation, he decided to move closer and take a better look. Testing each board before putting his full weight on it, he carefully made his way to the edge of the hole. Once there, he peered into it only to find the river raging a good distance below. Next, he moved to the sides of bridge and looked up and down the river but saw no sign that anyone or anything lived there. Finally, he went back to the hole, and in a rather timid voice, he asked, "Is anybody there?"

He didn't really expect a reply. Thus, he was terribly surprised and frightened when he heard a loud, booming voice yell, "GO AWAY!" He was so startled that he fell backward and landed squarely on his backside. For a moment, he remained there, more out of shock than injury. Once composed, he scampered to his feet and began to move quickly off the bridge. He was halfway up the hill when he was struck with the notion that he should at least say "thank you" because, most likely, this creature had saved his life. He turned around and marched back down to the bridge. At the foot of the bridge, he yelled "thank you," and then he placed his sack lunch on the ground before turning and leaving again. He moved slowly, hoping to hear a reply, but none was had. At the top of the hill, he paused and looked back over the valley, burning its image into his mind before returning home.

That night as he lay in bed and reflected over the day's events, he had an idea. The following morning, he packed another sack lunch and headed toward the bridge again. As he suspected, the sack lunch from the previous day was gone. Without saying a word, he put the new sack lunch on the ground in the same spot and then left. Every day that week, he returned to the bridge after school, performing the same routine. On several days, he had to go without lunch himself as there wasn't enough for them both, but this he gladly did. After about two weeks, his diligence was rewarded, and he finally got a response, albeit small. The response was a short message at the sack lunch drop-off site. Etched in the mud, Brad found the words, "YUR WELCUM." Grinning from ear to ear, Brad placed the sack lunch on top of the writing in the mud and then returned home. But on this trip home, his heart was too full to merely walk. Instead, he skipped, whistled, and sang the entire way.

With his debt paid, he could have stopped his daily pilgrimages to the bridge. He wasn't required to continue giving his time or food. But rather than stop, the response only invigorated his efforts. In addition to leaving food, he began to leave some of his most valued possessions. Every day, he happily parted with items such as comics, candies, and toys, and these also disappeared with the sack lunches each day. He had given away most of his possessions when he finally got the response that he had been hoping for. Following his usual routine, he quietly walked up to the bridge, left the food and loot on the ground, and then turned to walk away. But on this day, he was stopped in his tracks by a voice that said, "What's your name?"

Overwhelmed with excitement, Brad wheeled around and went over to the hole in the bridge. Once there, he nervously replied, "Brad…my name is Brad."

"That's a nice name," replied the voice in a slow, sad tone.

After the reply, there was a long and somewhat uncomfortable silence. He hadn't prepared for this moment, so he didn't have a statement to make or a list of questions to ask. In fact, he had never been good at small talk. Flustered, the only thing that he could think to say was what he had just heard. Like a parrot, he blurted out the same question that had been posed to him. "What's your name?" he asked.

There was a short pause before the creature from underneath the bridge replied. "My name...oh, you want to know my name? It's been a long time since someone has wanted to know my name. Well, I have been called many things but my true name is Denese."

"Denese...hmm...that is a good name. I doubt that I will be able to forget that one," said Brad. Almost immediately, laughter could be heard coming up through the hole in the bridge. "What's so funny? Did I say something wrong?" Brad asked.

Once Denese had finished laughing, she replied to his question. "No, you haven't said anything wrong. It's just that for most of my life others have simply forgotten about me...except for you it seems."

"What about your mother? Did she want to forget about you too?"

"Sadly, I never met her. She died giving birth to me. It was my father who named me. In his eyes, I was the cause of her death, and for that reason he hated me. He couldn't stand the sight of me because I was a continual reminder that she was gone, and he just wanted to forget that it ever happened...forget that I was ever born."

"I am very sorry that your father felt that way about you."

"That's OK. It was a long time ago," Denese said with a sigh.

As they spoke, Brad realized that they had something in common. They had both suffered greatly at the hands of their parents. Denese had been rejected by her father. He had been physically and verbally abused by his, and now he was being neglected by his mother. Tragedy in the form of broken relationships had struck them both. It had scarred their past, and to some extent, it subsequently was shaping their present and future. Collectively, it could be said that they shared a painful past, a less than perfect present, and a dubious future, but somehow, amid all of his pain and suffering, Brad found some solace in knowing that he was not alone in his plight. Feeling a great deal more comfortable with Denese and the situation at the bridge, he proceeded to blurt out a string of questions in rapid-fire succession like, "So what happened? What did you do? Where is your father now? Why do you live under a bridge?" But no reply was to be had. Only sniffling could be heard from under the bridge. Apparently, his questioning had forced Denese to reminisce about her past, and this process had exposed some wounds that had remained unhealed. Denese's laughter turned out to be short-lived, providing only a momentary respite from the pain that she felt in her heart. Brad could empathize, so he didn't badger her with any further questions. He remained quiet, patiently waiting for a reply if there was to be one. But no reply came. Realizing that their conversation had concluded, Brad turned and walked away, but not before he said, "Denese, it was very nice to finally meet you. I hope to continue our conversation tomorrow."

The walk home passed quickly as his mind was preoccupied with the happenings at the bridge. After many weeks, he had finally earned the right to be heard. The conversation was brief yet very meaningful. He had learned a name and the beginning of a story. Sadly, he realized that Denese's pain had begun at her birth. She had never gotten to experience any of the joys of youth. For her, there had never been any "good ol' times." As Brad considered this, he became very thankful for the time in his own life when he had been able to live in a state of blissful ignorance. He was also thankful, although somewhat grudgingly, for the life lesson that he had just been taught; the one that reminds you that when life seems bleak there is always someone who is far worse off than yourself. Brad had food, clothing, and shelter. Denese had none of these. This discrepancy grieved Brad deep down to his soul, and the anguish that it produced ignited a desire within his heart. In Denese, he felt a common bond, and he suspected that over time he would discover that they had much more in common. They both shared pain and loss. Collectively, these experiences created a great need, and from it, a desire was born. It was a new need; not one that took but one that gave instead. He had developed a need and desire to give, and although he did not know it at the time, his motivation was purely out of love.

THREE

To his surprise, Brad discovered his mother's car parked in the driveway when he got home. He quietly slipped inside hoping to go undetected, but his mother was already waiting for him in the kitchen. For a solid minute, she berated him for leaving the house without first asking permission. After the tongue-lashing had ended, she proceeded to tell him that his Aunt Margaret had passed away and that they would be leaving straightway to attend the funeral in Fun Town. Brad desperately tried to convince his mother that he should stay and look after things, but every excuse that he conjured up was immediately rejected. In the end, he had no choice in the matter. He had to go. After a quick packing job, he got into the car, and they sped away.

There were many reasons why Brad didn't want to attend the funeral, and none of them had to do with his aunt. Aunt Margaret, also known as Auntie M, was the firstborn and therefore oldest sibling in his father's family. Brad's father, George, was born much later, and by this time Auntie M was a teenager. According to Auntie M, she had practically raised his father. But, she had been so busy caring for everyone else that she had failed to look after herself. She had always been short and heavyset, but over the last few years, she had allowed herself to become morbidly obese. Despite the deterioration of her physical body, she had maintained a heart of gold. Most of his father's family had been relatively ambivalent in their treatment of him; that is, up until his father's incarceration. Since then, they treated Brad with contempt and scorn. For reasons that he didn't understand, part of the blame for his father's incarceration had been placed on him. The feelings that resulted had created an even further division between them. But not Auntie M—she had always treated him kindly. She had always welcomed him with open arms. Over the years, he had grown to love her. Now she was gone, and he felt like an abandoned soldier entering enemy territory to mourn over the dead body of a trusted ally.

But his primary apprehension about leaving Happyville had nothing to do with his father's family. He was more concerned about not being able to make it to the bridge the following day. He realized that he had just made a major breakthrough with Denese, and he had hoped that their relationship might grow from this victory. Now he feared that any progress that he had made up to this point would be lost if he couldn't return quickly. Brad knew that Denese had been rejected most of her life. Therefore, he worried that Denese might misunderstand his absence at the bridge and tally it as the newest entry in a long line of personal rejections. So, Brad was dually conflicted as his mother motored toward his aunt's funeral and away from Denese and the bridge.

Several hours later, they finally arrived at their destination. The scene at Auntie M's house was definitely something to behold. Cars and trucks lined the road for a least half a mile in both directions. While his mother searched for a suitable parking place, he watched as people came and went carrying boxes of food and bouquets of flowers. Some of the people he recognized, but many he did not, and those that he did not recognize he assumed to be friends and not family. Once his mother had found a place to park, they exited the car and walked up to the front door together. Brad was quite nervous about entering his aunt's home as he didn't know what type of welcome to expect, but once inside, he found the house to be very crowded and full of activity. He was reminded that his father was one of eight children and that his grandparents were also members of large families. As he made his way through the house, it seemed to him that most of the family was present and accounted for, and with some effort they had managed to pack themselves into his aunt's home much like sardines are packed into a can. To his relief, his arrival had gone seemingly unnoticed. He surmised that this was largely due to the size of the crowd but also due to the fact that everyone seemed to be busy doing something. He had chosen to lag far behind his mother so that those who did take notice of him might not make the connection that she was his mother and subsequently that George Buerger was his father. His strategy proved a success as he traversed the distance between the front and back door without being stopped. He remained at the back door only for a moment. As fortune had it, someone happened to be entering the house, and while the back door was open, he quietly slipped outside unnoticed.

The environment in the backyard contrasted greatly to the one that he had just left. Compared to the busyness within house, the backyard seemed desolate. As far as he could tell he was alone, and he hoped that for the foreseeable future he would remain this way. He realized that he would soon be discovered unless he found a suitable place to hide, so he began exploring the backyard, looking for a good spot. For the most part the backyard was bare, but there was a small, stand-alone shed in the right-hand corner of the yard that drew his attention. He quickly made his way there, opened the door, and slipped inside.

After his eyes had grown accustomed to the low lighting, he began to snoop around the shed. He had been looking for a hiding spot, but instead he found something that immediately caught his attention. It was a brand new bike. The bike was painted a brilliant red color and across the side the words, *Radio Flyer*, were written in white lettering. In Brad's eye, it was a thing of beauty. He had always wanted a bike. Over the years, he had ridden others' bikes, but he had never known the joy of owning his own. He had begun to believe that he would never know this joy. Tormented, he stood by the bike that was so close yet so far away. He dared not touch it lest he fall in love with something that he could not possess, but the longer he gazed over the red paint and shiny chrome, the more that he began to covet it. He had experienced so much pain over the last year, and somehow it seemed that through this bike, he might find some comfort. His mind began to whirl, and his convictions weakened. He was about to hop on and take a seat when a voice from behind him broke the trance that held him prisoner.

The voice said, "She's a beauty ain't she." Startled, Brad crashed into the bike and almost toppled over it. "Sorry, didn't mean to spook you," said the voice. Once steadied, Brad turned to discover Mr. Johnson sitting in a chair over in the corner. Brad began to blush when he realized that Mr. Johnson had been watching him the whole time. Brad watched as he slowly rose from his place. His thin, wiry, black frame creaked and popped as he got up from the chair and walked over to him. Brad had always thought Mr. Johnson and Auntie M were an odd couple, given the fact that he was so thin and she so fat, but for as long as he could remember, Mr. Johnson had lived at his aunt's house where it was his job to take care of her. Like his Auntie M, Mr. Johnson had always been kind to him. Thus, he figured that as far as the issue with his father went, he was probably either neutral or on his side. As Mr. Johnson neared him, he began to speak again. "I bet you were trying to get away from the crowd," he commented. Brad nodded his head. "Me too," he said as he methodically made his way over to the bike. Pointing to the bike, he said, "I always wanted a bike like this one when I was your age. But my family was just too poor. One day, I got the notion that I was just going to steal me a bike, and one day after school that is just what I did. I picked out a nice one, much like this bike here. I rode that bike home, but I hadn't figured out a good alibi, and my Pa saw right through me. He marched me right back up to that school and made return that bike and say that I was sorry, even though I didn't mean it. Then he took me home and wore my backside out. For that I was sure sorry."

Mr. Johnson paused for a moment to look Brad squarely in the eyes before continuing. "I'll bet you're wondering why I am telling you all this. Well, I guess it's because I saw that look in your eye; that's a look a man gets when he wants something so badly that he will do just about anything to get it. That was the same look that I had before I stole that bike. I wanted it so bad, and I let the thought of having it consume me. I allowed my own selfish desires lead me down a bad path. What I thought would bring me happiness only brought me pain. Learn from my mistake, son, and don't let your desires for things of this world destroy you like they have for so many. Now, you don't have a father anymore or a mother from what I understand to help guide you. At least, I had that. Nope, you're gonna have to do it on your own. You are going to have to be especially careful because the world is a dangerous place, and it will lure you into all sorts of traps...traps that cause pain, suffering, and even death."

At this point, Mr. Johnson turned back to the bike and ran his fingers over the handlebars. Then he gave out a long whistle and said, "She sure is something. You'd better take good care of her." Confused, Brad's eyes shot from the bike to Mr. Johnson's face. Grinning, he continued, "Why she's all yours. Your Auntie M had me go down to the store and pick her out a few weeks ago. It's your birthday present. Now go on and see how she feels." Brad wasn't quite sure if he really believed the whole thing, but Mr. Johnson continued to nod his head and motioned for him to get on the bike, so he did. Excitement flooded over him, and as he sat upon the bike, he felt a sensation of empowerment. He also felt something that he hadn't felt in quite some time...happiness. It wasn't just because he was a proud owner of a new bike; it was because someone, namely his Auntie M, had cared enough to remember his birthday, which was now only days away. Unable to contain himself, he hopped off of the bike and gave Mr. Johnson a big hug, which was duly reciprocated.

* * * *

Over the next couple of days, Brad was ushered from one place to another as he accompanied his mother wherever she went. Time and time again, he was introduced to various members of his father's family. As one might expect, this completely destroyed the anonymity that he had enjoyed at his Aunt's house, and by the time of her funeral, everyone knew who he was. He was pleasantly surprised to find that no one seemed to think ill of him. In fact, it was just the opposite. Everyone had been exceedingly kind to him throughout his stay. As Brad reflected over his time there, he realized that the funeral had been pivotal in making this unexpected outcome possible. If he had come to Fun Town under any other circumstance, the outcome would have probably been much different. The death of his Auntie M had done something that he had not anticipated. Her funeral had softened their hearts. It had also provided an opportunity for them to learn the truth about his father's case. They discovered that a few rumors had greatly distorted the truth. They learned that Brad had done no wrong. As a result, they began to see the wrong that they had been doing to him in both their thoughts and actions. Many said aloud that they were sorry, and although not spoken, many more said that they were sorry through their actions, and to all those who asked, forgiveness had been granted. They had come to him, many with tear-stained eyes, with their guilt weighing heavy on them, but through a seemingly simple act, they had left changed. They had been exonerated.

Their guilt had been washed away, and they had finally found peace. For Brad, a change of a different sort was occurring inside. From his father's family, he found the love that he had so desperately needed, and as a result, his tender heart began the long but much needed journey towards healing.

It was truly an interesting twist of fate. He had come to mourn the loss of his aunt. He expected to be treated poorly by his relatives, but he did not find this to be the case at all. Instead, he experienced something far different. In the most unlikely of places and at the most unlikely of times, he found redemption. Death had brought life, and what should have caused suffering had brought healing. In a million years, Brad could have never expected such an outcome. But, he understood that this outcome had come at a heavy price, and this price had been his aunt's life. It was only through her death that any of this had been made possible.

On the third day of their trip, they packed up their belongings in preparation for the trek home. Brad grinned as they pulled out of his aunt's driveway. Things had not gone as he had expected. His imagination had once again gotten the better of him. It had told him lies that he had believed as truth when, in reality, those things had been very far from the truth as he would ultimately discover. The morning in which they left a crowd had gathered. They didn't come with hate in their hearts as a lynch mob might, but instead they came out of love to wish both of them well. As they said their goodbyes, tears of joy were shed, and hugs given. Both sides agreed to do better by one another. Finally they promised never to forget the happenings surrounding Auntie M's funeral and the small miracle that had ensued.

FOUR

The return trip from Fun Town to Happyville seemed to pass painfully slow, but it wasn't because the trip had actually taken a longer increment of time, because it hadn't. Rather, it was because Brad was very eager to get home so that he could ride his new bike. The anticipation of riding it for the first time was almost more than he could bear. The feelings that stirred within reminded him of those that he typically felt on Christmas Eve. On those evenings, he usually slept poorly, tossing and turning in his bed as he kept a watchful eye on the clock. In a similar fashion, he fidgeted in his seat the entire way as he anxiously watched for road signs leading home. Every so often he would peek over his shoulder to gaze at the bike neatly packed in the backseat.

For the most part, Brad spent the trip daydreaming about the adventures that he would soon have while he was riding his brand new *Radio Flyer* bicycle. In his dreams, he embarked on daily quests, leaving the confines of Happyville to search out faraway and undiscovered lands. On his quests, he battled many foes and overcame countless obstacles as he trekked into the unknown. His adventures led him into many circumstances that were quite dire, but he always came out victorious in the end. Word of his courage and valor had spread far and wide, and as a result, he and his noble *Radio Flyer* had become the envy of all men. His daydreaming had succeeded in doing what he could not. It had taken him away from the depths of his current situation and put him into a far better place. In his dreams, he had undergone a transformation. He was no longer the court jester of Happyville. He had become one of the most renowned and respected knights in all of Happy Land. He knew that all of this had been made possible because of his new *Radio Flyer* bicycle.

With each passing mile, he became increasingly more excited. By the time they entered the city limits of Happyville, he was literally bouncing in his seat. When his mother pulled their car into the driveway, he jumped out while it was still moving. His mother was not pleased, and she let him know it, but her words only bounced off of him as he didn't care. His whole being had been consumed by the sole thought of the bike and his possession of it. Once his mother had finished reprimanding him, he ran back to the car, flung open the back door, and gently extracted his bike from the backseat.

On the driveway, he paused to admire its beauty one last time. In this moment, he took a mental snapshot of the brilliant red paint, shiny chrome, and black tires because he knew that soon it would be covered with dirt and mud. He would be able to clean it and make it like new, but it would never again be brand new. To this reality, he had begun to develop some mixed emotions. Part of him wanted the bike to remain just as it was in a perpetual state of being brand new. In this state, the bike had already brought him great joy, and he had found contentment in simply looking upon it with the realization that it was his and his alone. This part of him reasoned that he could put it away in his room for safekeeping where he could enjoy it for many years to come. The other part of him, the adventurous part, wouldn't stand for this, and ultimately, it won out.

With his decision firmly made, he mounted the bike, gripped the handlebars, and put his feet on the pedals. Then he pushed off and began coasting down the driveway. As he went, the wind and rain hit against his face. In the background, he heard his mother's voice. She was beckoning him to return for his raincoat, but he didn't stop and very quickly her voice faded away. He peddled his bike up a large hill, which he crested and then sped down the other side. As he raced down the hill, he was filled with a sensation of exhilaration. In this moment, everything that had been bothering him was washed away, and all that remained was his bike and the open road that lay before them.

* * * *

That night, he returned cold, wet, exhausted and extremely happy. He carefully cleaned off his bike with soap and water before storing it safely in the garage. Once inside, he was sent straight to the bathtub by his mother. After bathing and dressing, he was lured to the kitchen by the aroma of food. He found dinner waiting on him when he arrived. Like old times, he sat with his mother and ate a hearty dinner. Afterwards, he cleaned the dishes, kissed his mother's cheek, and went straight to bed where he quickly fell sound asleep.

The following morning, he awoke refreshed. He dressed and quickly ate breakfast before heading to the garage to gather his bike. This time, he remembered to take his raincoat before leaving. He spent the entire weekend riding his bike back and forth around Happyville. As he rode around the town, he happened upon several of his classmates. Each time, he was quick to stop and show them his new bike. From their reactions, he concluded that they were envious, which only fed the pride that had started growing in his heart. The following week, he rode his new bike to school where he showed it off to anyone that would give him a moment of their time.

But by the end of the week, his thoughts and feeling about his bike had begun to change. His classmates had quickly lost interest in him and his new bike. Thus, nothing had really changed at school. At home, his mother had started becoming more reclusive. Her crying spells had resumed. She had also started leaving early and coming home late again. Thus, he found that nothing had really changed at home either. He was once again alone. He still had his bike, but he had begun to tire of riding it from dawn to dusk. Despite his best effort, he had failed to find even the slightest adventure. None of his dreams had come to pass. Sadly, he realized that he was still just a lowly court jester. In disgust, he looked at his bike. He realized that he had put far too much faith in it. He had hoped that it would provide him lasting happiness, but it had only provided false hope and temporary happiness. He had only wanted to slip away from the reality of his situation, and the bike had enabled him to do so briefly. But eventually, his dreams were discovered for what they were. They were merely figments of his imagination and nothing more. In the end, he realized that the bike was just an object. It had no power of its own. It was not an end in itself but only a means to an end. It was only a tool that was meant to be used and not worshiped.

Dejected, he sought the confines of his bedroom where he sat and watched it rain. As he sat, boredom overcame him and with it came the sensation of sleepiness. He went over to his bed and plopped down on it. While laying there, the words of the sage, Mr. Johnson, echoed in his mind. He had warned him to beware of falling in love with such things, but despite his warning, he had done it anyway. He had not meant to ignore his advice. What had resulted was completely unintentional. The thoughts and feelings that had consumed him had crept upon him insidiously, and before he knew it, they had taken hold of him. In retrospect, he realized that he had thought about little else over the last couple of weeks. In particular, he had completely forgotten about Denese and the friendship that had been growing. He feared that his neglect might have caused irreparable damage. This thought greatly disturbed him, and it only added to the mounting self-condemnation that he already felt.

That evening, he skipped dinner because he wasn't all that hungry. He slept poorly, and several times he got up to pace the room because his mind wouldn't let him rest. Inside, a war was being waged. He felt guilty and stupid for his actions, and these feelings were beginning to drag him back into the abyss of his depression. He desperately didn't want to give into these feelings, but as the night drew on, the battle grew more intense. In the wee hours of the morning, he began to wonder if he would make it to see daylight. He had almost given up hope when the sun finally appeared. Upon seeing it, his mind and soul were immediately refreshed. Physically, his body was still tired and needed rest, but he knew that this would have to wait because, now that he was in the light of day, he could see what he had to do. The light had brought forth an idea, or solution, if you will. In this moment, he realized that he wasn't supposed to continue wallowing in his own self-pity. Rather, he needed to go and ask for forgiveness from Denese, for like everyone else, he had been guilty of forgetting about her. He just hoped that Denese could find it in her heart to forgive him. If she would, perhaps their relationship could be restored just as his relationship with his father's family had been. He knew that his plea might be refused, but as he thought about his options, he realized that he had nothing to lose and everything to gain.

FIVE

In the Buerger household, the concept of forgiveness had not been something that was routinely practiced or taught. Why that had been he didn't exactly know, but he suspected that at the heart of the matter, pride had been involved. His father, in particular, had always been a very proud person. He hated to ask for help because in his mind it meant that he was weak. But he had a greater flaw—he adamantly refused to admit that he had ever done anything wrong. Similar to asking for help, to him the admission of guilt was also a sign of weakness. On a deeper level, it seemed to Brad that his father feared admitting wrongdoing because in doing so, the façade that he had erected around himself might collapse. On the outside, his father projected himself as being strong and unflappable, but on the inside, he was altogether something different. Before the rain started, Brad would catch glimpses of what lay below the surface. Within the confines of their home, he would often catch his father crying. He was prone to mood swings and bouts of irritability. In retrospect, his father's entire life had been held together in a fragile balance. His persona was intimately wrapped in a construct of his own making, and anything that undermined that construct was a threat, because if it ever fell apart, then he would be exposed to the harsh reality that he had not been the person who he believed he was. This reality was something that his father didn't want to face. His pride was part of his armor, and the inability to admit wrongdoing and ask for forgiveness was a natural attribute of his armor.

But then the rain came and eroded the foundation of his barrier—his ability to provide—and to this attack his father had no defense. When his foundation finally collapsed, he collapsed with it. With nowhere to turn, he looked to alcohol to bury his pain, but this hadn't been enough and so he turned to abuse in attempt to transfer his pain elsewhere. As one might expect, this ended rather poorly. Brad didn't want to follow in his father's footsteps. He had been wrong, and he wasn't about to let his pride stand in the way of reconciliation. Two weeks ago, he had been on the receiving end of many requests for forgiveness. The table had turned, and now he would be the one asking for forgiveness. He only hoped that Denese would be as gracious as he had been.

He dressed for the day and then went to the kitchen for breakfast and to pack a lunch for her. He was in the process of leaving when an idea popped into his head. It was a simple idea for a gift that he could leave with the lunch. It would only require a piece of ribbon and a little effort on his part. After rummaging through his mother's sewing kit, he found a portion of what he needed. Then he went to the garage and got his bike. On this day, he was able to manage a smile at the sight of it. It was definitely going to make the long treks to the bridge a great deal easier. The night before, he realized that he had put many unrealistic expectations upon his bike, but today, he saw that it was going to serve a purpose after all. It was going to provide him quick and easy transportation to the bridge.

As he rode in the coolness of the morning, Brad felt raindrops on his face. High above him, a fine mist had started falling from the sky. Along the way, he stopped to pick some daffodils and tulips that were blooming on the side of the road. As soon as he had gathered enough, he neatly wrapped the ribbon around them forming a nice bouquet. At the foot of the bridge, he yelled out for Denese, but he wasn't surprised when he didn't hear a response. Then he laid the lunch and the bouquet of flowers at the foot of the bridge, and in the mud next to them, he wrote the words, "I am sorry." With his task finished, he got back on his bike and made the return trek home. It was out of his hands now. It was Denese's turn to respond, and Brad hoped with all of his heart that she would respond favorably.

Rather quickly Brad discovered that he would have rather been on the side of granting forgiveness than asking for it. On his previous encounter with forgiveness, he had been in control, but in this case, he found that he was at the mercy of someone else. He didn't like this feeling, and as a result, he spent most of the day moping around the house. He tried to focus his thoughts elsewhere but had great difficulty in doing so. By mid-afternoon, he was back on his bike riding out to the bridge to see if Denese had responded to his peace offering. As he neared the bridge, his heart began beating rapidly in his chest. He could tell that the lunch and bouquet of flowers he had left earlier in the day had been removed, but in their place, a white object now rested. From his vantage point, he wasn't quite sure what had replaced them, but he was eager to know. He sped up his pace, and in a matter of moments, he had successfully closed the gap. He quickly dismounted from his bike and went to the object for a closer inspection. He discovered that it was a dogwood tree branch. He carefully picked it up to examine it further. It was completely covered with a mass of beautiful white flowers. Each flower had four large petals joined together in such a way that they gave the appearance of a cross. While he held it, some of the petals fell off the branch. He watched them float softly to the ground, landing upon an inscription in the mud. Upon closer inspection, he found that the words "I am sorry" had been wiped away, and in their place the words "For Given" had been written. Immediately, a wave of relief washed over him. Then a smile broke across his face. The weight that had been sitting heavy on his heart had been lifted. His burden was now gone. He moved over to the hole in the bridge and shouted, "Hello…Denese…are you there?"

"Yes…Brad…I am here."

"Denese, I'm very sorry. I didn't mean to forget about you. So much has happened lately. I'm afraid that I just got distracted, but I promise not to let that happen again."

"That's OK," replied Denese.

"No, it's not OK. You saved my life. You deserve better."

"You don't know what I deserve," barked Denese. "You don't even know me! You don't know what I have become. You don't know that I am a vile creature who only deserves to die. In fact, I was trying to end my life the day that you fell through this bridge. I had thrown myself into the river miles upstream, but instead of drowning, I only washed up under this accursed bridge. So don't tell me what I deserve!"

Dumbfounded by Denese's words, Brad collapsed onto one of his knees. His mind was reeling from the information that he had just heard. Denese had apparently tried to kill herself on the same day and in the same manner that he had. The enormity of this revelation sent a chill down his spine. Eerily, he realized that they were more alike than he had previously thought. They had similar pasts that had placed them in the same location for the same reasons. They had looked for love and acceptance but had found none. Discouraged by their fruitless searching, they eventually came to a place of complete and utter despair. Once there, they stopped searching for these things and instead began searching for a way to escape from their misery. Then they stumbled upon the river, and in it they believed that they had found a solution. It was to be a fitting ending, especially for Brad since the vast majority of his problems had started with the rain. It was to be a river leading to death or, putting it another way, a river of death. But at the last moment, something unexpected occurred. They plunged into the river seeking death and found something entirely different. They found that their paths didn't end but crossed. In another interesting twist of fate, they discovered that the river of death had become a river of life. Death was not to be found in its waters on that day. It was just the opposite. Life had come as a replacement, miraculously springing forth from death itself.

Brad remained silent, kneeling at the edge of the hole in the bridge. He was too amazed to speak. Nor did he know what to say for that matter. Eventually, Denese broke the silence. "Brad, are you still there?'

Brad's mouth had become quite dry, making it very difficult to reply to her question, but after a few attempts, he was able to force out a "yes" in response.

"Brad…I'm sorry. You didn't deserve that."

Somewhat sheepishly, Brad replied by saying, "You don't know what I deserve." For a moment, there was silence, and then they both erupted into laughter. Once they had quieted down, Brad spoke again. This time, he was deathly serious. "Denese, I came to the bridge to end my life too, and I would have succeeded if it weren't for you, but thankfully, you saved me. Now I realize that it was a mistake. So again, I tell you that I am very grateful. I also realize that I can never fully repay you, but if you would let me, I would like to start by being your friend."

"I would like that very much, but I don't believe that is possible."

"I don't understand?"

"You don't know what I am, and I fear that once you see me that you will change your mind."

Confused, he said, "I'm sorry Denese, but I don't understand."

With a sad voice, Denese continued, "Brad, I'm not like you. Let's just say that I am different. I believe that if you saw me for who I truly am that you would be frightened."

"Denese, I would like to make that decision myself. May I come down? I would like to see you. I don't believe that you are as bad as you think."

"Brad, please don't come down. If you really want to be my friend, then don't ask to see me. I would prefer it that way. The truth is that you belong up there, and I belong down here under this bridge."

"Denese, I don't fully understand, but maybe one day I will. For now, I will do as you wish."

Denese responded by saying, "Thank you," and for the next couple of hours, they sat and talked as if they were old friends. Brad sat with his legs hanging down through the hole in the bridge, and Denese remained hidden out of sight. They found that they very much enjoyed the other's company. When the light of day began fading, they said their goodbyes, and then Brad slowly made his way back home. He had a great deal to ponder on his return trip. On this day, he had once again experienced the power of forgiveness, except on this occasion, he was not the one granting forgiveness but the one receiving it. It was an entirely different perspective when compared to his last encounter, but the ultimate outcome had essentially been no different. The end result was healing and restoration of a relationship.

The afternoon had also brought forth a couple of additional surprises. In a startling revelation, he realized that their lives had been brought together through a series of unrelated, but eerily similar events. When considered in context, the manner in which their first day at the bridge had unfolded was truly amazing. If the timing had been off by even one hour, they may have never met. Even more sobering was the fact that he probably would not still be alive. They were seemingly random events, yet when examined as a whole, they fit together almost too perfectly to be mere coincidence. However, because he had no other working hypothesis, he was left with the conclusion that the events of that day had happened by chance. Finally, he had succeeded in befriending Denese. He would be the first to admit that it was a rather odd arrangement, but for the time being, it was an arrangement that seemed to work for them. Denese's desire to remain hidden had given him an intense feeling of curiosity. He couldn't help but wonder what secret she was hiding. He had never seen any part of her, and he wondered if he ever would. Similarly, he wondered if Denese would ever change her mind and allow herself to be seen. But at the same time, he questioned whether he truly wanted to see her at all. This part of him reasoned that maybe Denese was only trying to protect him from some unimaginable horror. Even at the relatively young age of twelve, he realized that the world was a harsh place, and as such, there were some things that were best left unseen.

SIX

When Brad left for the bridge, faint gray clouds had filled the sky. As a whole, this finding was not a surprise because these clouds had become somewhat of a staple for the town of Happyville; nor was it a surprise to the type of clouds that filled it. These faint gray clouds had provided the backdrop for the long winter months, and they had added to the mundane nature of winter in the sense that they never changed. When one arose in the morning, the clouds were there, and when one went to sleep in the evening, they were there as well. From day to day, their color and character never changed. The amount of precipitation that they produced was the only variable. Some days, it rained very little, and on others, there was a deluge. But one could never deduce the amount based on the appearance of the clouds alone, for they never changed, or so it seemed.

For the record, this particular day had begun just like any other. As usual, the sky had shown forth with the color of a melancholy gray. The precipitation had been slight, and there was little if any wind blowing. For the vast majority of the day, it had remained just this way, but as Brad began his return trek home from the bridge, something unusual began to occur. The clouds in the sky, the ones that had remained unchanged for many months, began changing. At first glance, he was rather skeptical, believing that his eyes had deceived him somehow, but upon closer inspection, he realized that his eyes had not fooled him.

Change was occurring, and it was happening rapidly. The light gray clouds were quickly being overtaken, and in their place, dark, ominous-looking clouds were gathering. Their presence sent off warning signals in the back of his mind, because he feared that they might be thunderclouds. When a flash of lightning streaked across the sky, he realized that his fears were confirmed and that the system blowing in was indeed an electrical storm, the very first of the year.

It had been many months since an electrical storm had passed over the town of Happyville, and for this storm-free period, he had been very grateful. In their area, electrical storms were notorious for their severity, and from an early age, Brad had developed a healthy respect for lightning. It began at the age of four when he watched his neighbor's home burn to the ground after being struck by a bolt of lightning. Following this encounter, he began to closely observe how electrical storms affected the lives of others in his town. With each passing year, he noted each new victim that it tallied. This awareness only increased his respect for these storms. Over the years, he discovered that lightning was not the only weapon in the storm's arsenal. Some of the storms brought flooding rains and high winds that could also create a great deal of damage. But there was something even more dreaded than these, and that was the occasional tornado which had been known to show up without warning and wreak complete and utter havoc on the whole town.

So, with the first electrical storm of the year bearing down upon him, he felt an urgent need to get home as quickly as possible. He tightened his grip on the handlebars and started peddling with all his might. In only a moment's time, the bike was zooming down the road at full speed. Underneath him, the tires produced a whizzing sound as the water from the road sprayed against his body. On this afternoon, he didn't take any extra time to circumvent some of the larger puddles. Instead, he went down the middle of the road driving headlong into them. As he rode, he kept one eye on the road and one eye on the oncoming storm. He realized that he was on a collision course with it. He only hoped that he could make it home before they met. At ground level, there was still little, if any, sign of an approaching storm. There was no wind, and it was barely raining, but as the storm moved closer, this too began to change.

His initial encounter with the storm was with its wind. Before there were any visible signs of it, he felt its presence. The sensation was that of a warm, moist washcloth against his face. Following this, he began to see other signs of the wind, primarily in the trees surrounding him. The leaves on the trees began to nervously flitter to and fro, and as the wind strengthened, the trees themselves began to dance, swaying their branches back and forth in the air. Accompanying the wind were some large raindrops. They dropped like artillery shells out of the sky. Some splattered on his hands and arms and then a couple managed to hit him squarely in the face. He was in the storm clouds' sights, and at any moment, he knew that they would open their cargo doors to release their payload. Not wanting to be the victim of their bombing, he continued his frantic pace home, and to his relief, he made it just before the downpour began. In fact while he was storing his bike, a sea of large raindrops began falling from the sky. Almost instantly, the day was blotted out, and the night ushered in. From that point forward, the only light that remained came from the lightning that periodically streaked across the nighttime sky.

That evening in the safety of his home, Brad tried his best to follow his usual routine. However, he discovered that he was quite apprehensive about the storm that was raging all around him. His appetite was poor, and so he ate very little at dinner. In a similar fashion, he didn't feel like bathing so he hastened through this task as well. He also skipped books, and in their place, he chose to retire early to bed. After settling into his bed, his mind drifted back to Denese, and once there, he couldn't help but wonder how she was fairing on this night. He was very concerned for her well-being, and he hoped that she was safe underneath the bridge. In conjunction with this thought, he also thought about tomorrow, and he hoped that the storm would be gone by then so that he could venture out to see her again.

* * * *

In the wee hours of the morning, the storm's assault on the town of Happyville ended. For the townsfolk, the storm's arrival had been much like the arrival of an unwanted visitor. Filled with ill intent, the storm had crept into their town carrying weapons of destruction. Its rain had pounded their roofs, and for a few homes, it had successfully exposed leaks. In addition to the rain, the storm had also brought lightning, and for several hours it had struck violently, keeping most of the residents awake and cringing in their beds. But then the storm passed, departing just as suddenly as it had arrived, and in its absence the night underwent a transformation. With the thunder and lightning gone, the night turned pitch black and deathly quiet.

By this point in the night, the entire town of Happyville, minus one notable exception, had drifted off into a deep sleep. While the rest of Happyville rested peacefully in their beds, Brad struggled mightily to join them. In an attempt to get comfortable, he kept shifting positions in bed. The harder that he tried to fall asleep the more difficult the task became. This was partially due to the fact that he had grown accustomed to the lullaby of crickets chirping and frogs croaking, but on this night, they weren't playing their age-old tunes. In their absence, no other sounds filled the night. As the hours passed, the continued silence increased his restlessness all the more.

As Brad lay awake, his mind began to wander. Beginning

with his father's change in character, he moved forward in time, reflecting over some of the darker moments from his recent past. If at all possible, he tried to keep memories such as these locked away in the deep recesses of his mind. In fact, he tried to avoid them altogether because he feared that if he pondered them too long, he might inadvertently release them. So strong was his aversion for these memories that on a few occasions he had even tried to wish them away, but experience had taught him that this was a futile effort. Thus, they remained, looming like dark shadows in the far corners of his mind.

There were many reasons why he wished that he could forget these particular memories, and at the root of each was the feeling of fear. If history had taught him anything, it was that once released these memories would ravage his mind, tearing it apart. Therefore, he was deathly afraid to ponder them. To protect himself from venturing down this dead-end path, he had subconsciously placed roadblocks along the way, but on this night, exhaustion had gotten the better of him. As such, he failed to heed their warnings. By the time he realized what he had done, it was far too late. His mind had drifted into a place where a darkness far greater than the night reigned.

With the door to his mind wide open, an oppressive spirit entered in unopposed. When this occurred, everything changed. His chest felt heavy as if a large weight had suddenly been placed upon him. His heart began beating rapidly. His breath became short. These feelings created an overwhelming compulsion to move, so he sat bolt upright in bed. He kept gasping for air in an attempt to ease the horrible feelings that had built up inside, but to his dismay, the sensation only worsened. This precipitated a fear unlike any that he had ever experienced. In the back of his mind, a whispering voice told him that he was going to die.

With the prospect of death staring him in the face, he utterly panicked. He tried to flee from this unknown danger, but when he attempted to move, he found that he was powerless to do so. He felt like a deer in headlights because his mind and body were no longer functioning properly. The horrible feelings that were building up inside continued to mount. As he struggled, his world started spinning uncontrollably. A wave of nausea and a cold sweat broke over his body. At the apex of the attack, he actually wished that he might die so that his suffering would end.

But his wish did not come true, and he discovered that he had been left to languish in this awful state instead. Fear had paralyzed his physical body, leaving his soul scratching and clawing for a way out. He desperately wanted to rip open his skin so that his soul could escape from his tormented body. Despite his best effort, he quickly discovered that the harder he struggled to escape the worse his predicament became. In addition to being confused and scared, he was now frustrated. He attempted to vocalize his frustration by screaming. On his first attempt, he was only able to muster a faint whisper. On his second attempt, he took in a deep breath and then let it loose with every ounce of energy that he had. This time a loud, spine-tingling scream filled the room.

The act of screaming should have brought him some relief, but it hadn't. His uneasiness only increased. This was because he realized that he hadn't really screamed at all. Like his first attempt, he had only managed to force out a faint whisper. The scream that had resulted wasn't through his efforts. It had actually come from somewhere else, but where, exactly, he knew not. He surmised that it had to be close, possibly just outside his window. Focusing his eyes outside, he looked intently for any signs of movement. He peered into the pitch-black darkness but failed to detect any moving shapes or objects. As he kept watch, a second, blood-curdling scream echoed throughout the night. Once it had ended, the silence returned again. He remained motionless in his bed, but while waiting, he developed a foreboding sense that he was being watched. Then the hairs on the back of his neck stood straight on end.

He was once again overwhelmed with a sudden urge to flee for cover. When he tried to move this time, he discovered that his arms and legs were fully functional, so he moved to the floor and hid under the bed. While he lay on the floor contemplating his next move, a third scream filled the night. As he reflected over the screams, he began to notice a similarity between them. In fact, each scream sounded exactly the same. Each produced an awful, ear-piercing shrill of similar quality, tone, and length. In themselves, they were terribly frightening. However, with no other signs of impending danger, his fears began to abate, and in its place, his curiosity began to grow. He slowly poked his head out from under the bed, but from his vantage point, he failed to detect any signs of movement. At this point, it dawned on him that he was at the mercy of the night, and that if he was to ever discover the scream's source, he would need a light of some sorts.

The location of the closest flashlight just happened to be in a nearby desk, so he took in a deep breath and crawled to it. Hoping to remain out of sight, he slithered on the floor like a snake. Once there, he opened the top drawer and removed the flashlight. Then he quickly moved to the window and sat on the floor. After taking a moment to ready himself, he brought the flashlight up to his face with the intentions of turning it on. Before pressing the button, he took a hard swallow, realizing that he was about to give away his position. He knew that in the process of identifying himself that he might bring unwanted trouble upon himself, but his decision was already made. He flipped the switch on, and instantly the flashlight emitted a brilliant white light. With the flashlight in hand, he crawled onto his knees and began investigating. Directing the light back and forth across the yard, he searched the grounds immediately outside their home. After a quick pass, he discovered that nothing in the yard seemed out of place. Feeling more at ease, he continued his search by shining the light back and forth in an ever-enlarging arc. Eventually, he reached a point where the capabilities of the flashlight had been exhausted. With no sign of danger in sight, he breathed a sigh of relief and concluded his search.

As he turned off his flashlight, a fourth scream billowed into the night. Startled by the scream, he jerked away from the window. He tried to stop himself from falling backwards but was unable to do so. He fell onto his back, hitting his head in the process. This left the back of his head throbbing. His ears were also ringing from the sound of the last scream. After his wits returned, he reassessed the situation. Focusing on the last scream, he realized that it had come from a direction in which he had not looked. Previously, he had only searched the grounds outside of his home, but after this last scream, he realized that it had not come from the ground but from the sky. Looking through the window, he stared into the nighttime sky but saw nothing. Then he scrambled onto his knees and pointed the flashlight at the large oak tree that was located just outside his room. Starting at its trunk, he began moving upwards. After his search of the center of the tree came up empty, he began surveying its branches. Beginning with the lower branches, he started looking closely at each one. On the branch closest to his window, his search ended. On it, he found a pair of shining, yellow eyes, curiously looking upon him. Upon closer inspection, he discovered that they belonged to a small, white, feathered creature. Immediately, he recognized the creature as a screech owl. For the next minute, the owl sat on the branch staring at him. The only movement that it made during this time was to blink its eyes. While observing it, he couldn't help but notice that the owl seemed completely unafraid. After several more minutes past, he began to wonder if the owl would stay perched outside his window for the rest of the night. But then, without any warning, the owl emitted a final scream and flew away, leaving just as suddenly as it had arrived.

With the owl gone, Brad let out a sigh of relief. He had feared the worst, but in the end, he had discovered that his fears were again unfounded. He had expected to find something truly horrible, but in the end, he found that this wasn't the case at all. It turned out that his monster was only a cute, little owl. Yawning, he turned away from the window and put his back against the wall. As he rubbed his eyes, he hoped that there would be no more drama on this night. With the owl gone, he knew that there would be no more screams, and for this he was glad. Deep down, there was a part of him that hated to see his little friend fly away. He had given him quite a scare, but if truth be told, he had actually saved him from something far scarier. Prior to the owl's scream, he had been under attack by something that he was still trying to comprehend. The best way that he could describe it was that something had been imposing its will on him. It had entered his mind, and once there, it had begun to contort his thoughts by bending the truth into the form of lies. Eventually, the truth had been manipulated in such a way that it was being used against him, to condemn him.

For a moment, he had believed that he was actually going to die, but then the owl arrived. When it screamed, the trance that he had been under was broken. Then instead of focusing on himself, his attention had been drawn to the mysterious noise outside. In retrospect, he realized that when this occurred he had been freed from whatever was holding him. In yet another interesting twist of fate, he realized that something that had initially brought him great fear had actually saved him from the oppressive spirit that had been tormenting him. For this, he was very grateful, and he wanted to show his gratitude to his little friend, but he didn't know how. So he did the only thing that he could think to do. In the darkness of his room, he uttered a soft but audible "thank you" to his little friend, the guardian owl. After he had finished saying these words, he pushed himself up from the floor, went over to his bed, flopped down upon it, and quickly fell asleep.

SEVEN

Over the next several hours, Brad slept soundly in his bed. During this time, his movements were sparse, but on occasion, he would shift from side to side as he attempted to get into a more comfortable position. As a result, his blankets had been pulled loose from their original position, and instead of lying flat on his bed, they had become wrapped around his entire body, binding him tightly. In a curious sort of way, his appearance was quite similar to that of a cocoon. There was a layer of protection on the outside, and on the inside of this barrier of blankets, he snuggled like a bug, feeling very warm, cozy, and safe.

As a general rule, Brad was an early riser who liked to get out of bed at daybreak, but this day was different. Since he had not fallen asleep until the wee hours of the morning, he had decided to sleep in, and because the day of record was a Saturday, there was no reason why he couldn't. Besides, on Saturdays his mother left extra early for work. Thus, the atmosphere within the Buerger's home on Saturday mornings was usually one of peace and quiet.

* * * *

At the same time, in a location just south of Happyville, a flock of crows was approaching. They were traveling northbound, heading straight for the town. Riding on the wind, they came soaring high up in the sky. They quickly passed over Happyville en route to their final destination, the home of Brad Buerger. When they arrived, they quickly descended, landing on the roof and surrounding trees. The largest of the crows landed on Brad's windowsill. Once there, it began pecking on his window. The sound was literally unnerving, and in under a minute, Brad was forced from his slumber. He rolled over in bed to investigate the sound. After his eyes had adjusted, he saw the crow sitting upon the windowsill. He immediately noticed that this crow wasn't like most of the crows that he had seen. Compared to others, this crow was very large and menacing. Its body was covered with a layer of jet-black feathers, and as the morning light shone upon them, its coat began to shimmer. With Brad awake, the crow stopped his pecking and started inspecting him by turning its head from side to side while looking at him with its beady glass eyes. Angered that he had been awakened, Brad yelled, "Go away, stupid bird!" In response, the crow let out a loud call and then, like the owl from the previous night, flew away. However, unlike the owl, the crow didn't go very far. It simply joined the other crows in the trees, and together, they erupted into a chorus of their own calls.

Back inside the Buergers' home, Brad tried to fall back asleep, but the noise being generated by the crows outside made this impossible, so he decided to get up. He swung his legs off the bed and placed his feet firmly on the floor. While yawning, he stretched his arms above his head. A feeling of exhaustion fell over him. His head started throbbing, and his back began aching along the entire length of his spine. That's when he remembered his backwards fall in the early hours of the morning. He slowly got up and started his morning routine. In the kitchen, he rummaged for something to eat, but all that he could find was some moldy bread and rotten leftovers. When his search came up empty, he decided to forgo breakfast in lieu of visiting Denese at the bridge. In the wake of last night's storm, he was concerned about her safety. He grabbed his raincoat and exited through the front door. Then he pushed his bike to the driveway and mounted it. A twinge of pain shot down his back causing him to lose his balance momentarily. After steadying himself, he gingerly set off once again.

Rather quickly, he realized that there was something different about this day. His first clue was in how the air felt. It was heavy and oppressive, and in many ways, the sensation reminded him of a hot, humid summer day, but since it was still early April, he thought this quite odd. Casting his eyes overhead, he saw that the sky was its usual overcast gray. On occasion, a raindrop would fall from the sky and pelt against his raincoat. In addition to these signs, he also heard thunder periodically rumbling off in the distance. From the surface, nothing seemed all that different, but as he struggled to take in a deep breath, he knew that something had indeed changed. Soon his curiosity about the climate change faded, and he began to think about other things as he followed the well-worn path to the bridge.

After he had gone about a quarter of the way, he began to sense that he was being followed. However, when he looked back down the road, he saw that the roadbed was empty. A quick scan of the woods failed to detect anything noteworthy. Shrugging off this feeling, he continued on his course, but the suspicion that he was being followed only intensified. Looking back a second time, he saw that the roadbed was still empty, but out of the corner of his eye, he did notice that the sky overhead had darkened. It was no longer a shade of gray but black. In a millisecond, his mind processed the change and told him that bad weather was on the way. Then he assumed that the weather was the cause of the oppressive feeling and the notion that he was being followed. A warm front must be heading their way, bringing a storm with it. He began laughing at himself for behaving in such a silly manner. Feeling more reassured, he quickly pushed these worries out of his mind.

He continued on the path to the bridge, weaving in and out of mud puddles and passing old and familiar landmarks along the way. About halfway into his trip, a loud rumble of thunder pealed nearby. He looked to the sky once again and was shocked by what he saw. In disbelief, he kept staring, trying to comprehend the image that his eyes beheld. It was an image of a black sheet moving in the sky. Upon closer inspection, he realized that the black sheet was comprised of many smaller moving parts. Straining his eyes even further, he deduced that the smaller moving parts were actually birds flying in the air. In amazement, he realized that the scene before him was indeed a flock of birds, the largest that he had ever seen. He guessed that there must have been hundreds if not thousands of crows flying just above him. He was so enthralled with this sight that he failed to pay any attention to the road in front of him, and as a result, he drove his bike straight into a deep pothole. When this occurred, his front tire dug into it, and his bike came to a screeching halt. He was instantly propelled over the handlebars. When he came back down to the ground, everything went black. He wasn't sure how long he lay unconscious, but upon awakening, he was acutely aware of an intense aching on the right side of his face where a large abrasion had formed. Fortunately, he hadn't sustained any serious injuries, but the accident had only magnified the pain that he already felt in both his head and back. Gathering himself, he crawled onto his feet and went over to his bike. After a quick inspection, he determined that it too had weathered the accident without suffering any irreparable harm. Casting his eyes skyward, he saw that the sky had returned to its usual gray color. He looked for the crows but saw no further signs of them.

While mounting his bike, he noticed that the trees surrounding him had come to life and were nervously moving. Upon closer inspection, he realized that the trees themselves weren't actually moving. Rather the movements were coming from within the trees. They were full of birds. The very same crows that had been flying overhead were now in the trees that lined the road. As Brad grappled with this fact, he wondered if they might actually be following him. At first, he dismissed this fanciful idea as mere happenstance, but then he remembered that it had been a black crow that had rudely awakened him earlier in the morning. This revelation sent a cold chill down his spine and filled his belly with a foreboding feeling. Not wanting to remain there any longer, he quickly mounted his bike and took off down the road. In the background, he heard the crows calling to one another. The magnitude of their collective calls was almost deafening, and for quite some time, he continued to hear them call to one another in the background. He noticed that they sounded eerily similar to the sound of a laugh. In an attempt to banish the thought of them from his mind, he focused his full attention on the road before him. He poured the force of both his mind and body into peddling his bike because he wanted to get as far away from them as he could. When he could hear them no more, he turned back and scanned both the road and sky, and to his relief, he saw no further signs of them. However, when he turned and looked ahead, he did see something that made his heart sink with fear.

Over the last month, he had traversed the road to the bridge countless times without crossing paths with even a single person. But this was about to change, for just ahead of him, leaning against the sign that read "Bridge Closed–Dead End," was a man wearing a black hat and trench coat. Immediately, Brad had reservations about proceeding any further. He even considered turning around and going back home, but he dismissed this idea and continued onward with the hope that he could speed by the man and avoid any encounter at all. But, as he continued his approach, the man in black moved away from the sign and positioned himself in the dead center of the road. Then he lit up a cigarette, began to smoke it, and waited for Brad to come forward.

Brad came to a quick stop to review his options. As far as he could tell, there was no room to go around the man. He considered another route to the bridge, but he didn't know of one. Alternatively, he considered forgoing his visit to the bridge. He knew that this would be his easiest course of action. It would only take a moment for him to turn around and go back home, but as he contemplated this choice, he realized that it wasn't what he wanted. He had come to see Denese, and despite all that had already happened this morning, his desire hadn't changed. If he was to see her, he would have to go past the man in black.

With his decision made, Brad proceeded slowly. He didn't know what the man wanted, so he kept his distance. Brad brought his bike to a stop before reaching him. He put one foot on the ground and left the other on the pedal. He positioned himself so that he could flee quickly in the event that he needed to do so. He didn't know the man in black's intentions, but judging from his appearance, he assumed that they might not be good. Deep down, his instincts told him to beware of this man because he was bad to the core. This feeling put every fiber of his being on edge, and he readied himself to bolt at the first sign of danger.

Sensing Brad's uneasiness, the man in black took one last drag off his cigarette. Then he flicked it to the ground and crushed it under the heel of his boot. Next, he removed his hat, taking a moment to brush the dust away from the brim before placing it back on his head. Then he looked up at Brad and said in a rather pleasant voice, "Relax, my boy. I mean you no harm. In fact, I am only trying to help." After saying this, he paused for a moment to let Brad consider his offer. Meanwhile, Brad continued watching him like a hawk because he seriously doubted what the man had said was true. The man spoke up again, "I can see that you aren't too sure about me and that's okay. We don't have to be friends.

But I would like to offer you some advice, because if I don't, I fear that something bad might happen to you, and I wouldn't be able to forgive myself if I hadn't done all that I could to protect you." With the hint of danger looming, Brad turned to the man, giving him his full and undivided attention. Like before, the man paused to allow Brad to contemplate his last statement.

Brad's imagination began to run wild. He immediately feared the worst...that something terrible had happened to Denese. So great was this fear that he found that he was unable to contain himself. Thus, he blurted out in a rather distressed voice, "What do you mean?"

"Well for starters, the bridge is out. It's in bad shape and quite dangerous, and it's definitely no place for a young boy to play. You could get hurt, or even worse, you could be killed." Then the man grinned and said, "But I expect that you already knew that, didn't you." After saying this, he looked back and pointed at the sign. Then he took off his hat and held it in his left hand. "No, the reason that I'm here is because I wanted to warn you about what lives under the bridge." As he spoke, he used his hat as an illustration. He continued holding it in his left hand and then used his right hand to motion back and forth underneath it. Up to this point, Brad had been listening intently to the man in black, but when he made a negative reference about Denese, he began to question whether he had heard his last statement correctly. A look of confusion broke over his face. Realizing that he had Brad right where he wanted him, the man in black continued, "You need to know that there is a dangerous creature living under that bridge, and if you go down there, it will gobble you up because it loves to eat humans, especially little children."

Angered, Brad's face turned a bright shade of red, and then he yelled out, "That's a bold-faced lie! You're nothing but a liar! Denese would never eat me!"

"Oh...so you have met this creature. Well that means you're

either very brave or very foolish." He rubbed his chin while pondering which one. "I guess you may be a little bit of both. Nevertheless, I am surprised that you are still alive. I wonder why it spared you." He paused for a moment to consider his own question. Then he pointed his finger in the air and proclaimed, "I know. It's probably just waiting for the right occasion to eat you."

In defense of Denese, Brad exclaimed, "No, you're wrong! Denese would never eat another person."

"You speak as if this Denese were an actual person like yourself."

"That's because she is a person. I've spoken to her many times."

"Hmm…I wonder…have you ever seen this Denese?" Realizing that he hadn't, Brad sheepishly backed down. "I thought not," said the man. "There is a reason that she doesn't want you to see her, and it is because she isn't actually human. No, she is just a big, stupid, smelly troll."

Brad's brow furrowed, and then he said, "A troll…there are no such things! They're only imaginary creatures."

"Is that so? Hmm…I wonder…have you ever been to the North Country on the other side of the bridge, the place that your people have so appropriately named the Forgotten Land?" Brad shook his head signifying that he hadn't. "I thought not. Well, that is where Denese and her troll-kind roam."

"That's a lie. No one lives over there. Everyone knows that a terrible plague struck the land, killing all of the people that lived there. That was over a hundred years ago. It has been uninhabited ever since."

"Now that, my boy, is a lie. It is a lie that your grandparents told to your parents, and they in turn have passed it onto you. It is a lie that has been perpetuated for three generations, and it's been told for so long that it has now become truth. I know that it is a lie because I have been to the North Country and seen them. They are a foul and disgusting bunch. It's no wonder that the world has wanted to forget about them. But they are there all right. There is no denying that fact."

"Why...why would they tell us such a lie?"

"To protect you, my boy. Didn't you hear what I said? Trolls are dangerous. They couldn't have trolls running rampant throughout your land, and they couldn't have you going to explore theirs. The river has been a natural barrier for years because trolls can't swim, and they aren't smart enough to build a bridge or boat. The troll that is living under that bridge shouldn't be there. She must have fallen into the river. She should have drowned, but somehow she made it to the other side. Now this troll that you call Denese may seem nice, but that's just the human side of her coming out. She was probably weakened when she crossed the river. Who knows, she may even be sick. But she will get better, and when she does, her strength will return. Then she is going to get hungry, and I recommend that you be far away from this place when that happens."

"What do you mean...human side?"

The man continued, "At one time, they were like us, but then something happened to them. Something infected them, changing them. Now they are no longer fully human. They have become vile half-breeds, being both human and animal. Their human side is cunning, and I suspect that this Denese is only trying to lead you into a trap. And trust me when I tell you that you don't want to see their animal side because it will be the last thing that you see." After this last warning, the man in black pulled out another cigarette and placed it between his lips. Once lit, he took a long drag making the end of the cigarette glow orange. With the cigarette dangling between his lips, he motioned with his other hand and said, "Now go on and get out of here and don't come back. Just stay at home where it is safe. I know you don't understand this now, but one day you will, and when that day comes, you'll see that I was looking out for your best interests."

Realizing that he had no rebuttal for the man in black, Brad silently turned his bike around and began the long trek home. He wished that he had something smart to say in Denese's defense, but the man in black's accusations about Denese and the land north of the bridge had caught him completely off guard and left him bewildered. On the trip home, he busily contemplated all that he had been told. While reflecting over their conversation, he struggled with what was truth and what was a lie. He wondered if he should believe anything that he had been told. He had just met the man in black after all, and he really didn't know anything about him. All that he had was his first impression, and he had to admit that the man in black failed to strike him as being very trustworthy. However, the fact that Denese had never let herself be seen did make him wonder if he might be telling the truth at least partly, but which parts were true and which were false, he couldn't be certain. The most concerning aspect of the man's accusations against Denese was his portrayal of her as a savage beast who was capable of cold-blooded murder just for the sake of a meal.

EIGHT

Once home, Brad moped around the house looking for something, anything, to do. He desperately wanted to push the memory of the last hour from his mind, so he busied himself with doing chores around the house. After he had finished cleaning the house, he took a bath to clean himself. Then he collapsed on the couch, and for a few minutes he flipped through the channels on TV, but when he couldn't find anything worth watching, boredom quickly set in. Next, he tried to read a book, but he gave up on this when he realized that he had been reading the same sentence over and over again. When his stomach growled, he remembered that he had not eaten breakfast, and as the pantry was bare, he decided to treat himself for lunch. He scrounged together what money he could find, and then he headed off for the Happy Land Hamburger, one of his favorite fast food restaurants. With a burger, fries and a shake in his belly, he felt slightly better, but once the food euphoria had worn off, he found that his mind kept drifting back to the man in black. Their encounter kept repeating in his mind, and as these thoughts flooded over him, several feelings began bubbling up inside.

For reasons that he couldn't explain, he felt dirty as if he had done something wrong. He had tried cleaning his home to see if that might make him feel better, but when it didn't, he tried to clean himself instead. When this failed, he realized that there was nothing that he could do to make himself feel clean. He had no idea how long this feeling might last, but he hoped that it would pass quickly. In addition to this feeling, he felt confused because the man in black's words had left him not knowing what was true or false. Quite frankly, he didn't know what to believe. At the beginning of the day, he had no reason to believe that Denese wasn't his friend, but because of the man in black, he now had considerable doubts about her true intentions. Fear began creeping into his mind as well. When he thought about the man in black's features and mannerisms, he realized that he was deathly afraid of him. Likewise, as he thought about Denese and how little that he knew about her, he began to fear her also.

While pedaling home from the Happy Land Hamburger, he continued to contemplate the situation at the bridge, and after considering each side of the story, he formed a couple of conclusions. First, he realized that he couldn't trust either Denese or the man in black because he didn't have enough facts. Second, he realized that his encounter with the man in black had greatly affected his thoughts and emotions. He felt dirty, confused, and afraid. He knew that he didn't deserve to feel this way, because he hadn't done anything wrong. In fact, he had only been trying to help. He knew that his intentions for visiting the bridge had been both good and noble. The food, gifts, and time that he had given had been done purposefully. Through these acts, he had hoped to foster a friendship. He had also hoped that Denese might develop bigger dreams of her own. For instance, he hoped that Denese would leave her life of seclusion and come out from under the bridge. He dreamed of seeing Denese live a happy and productive life. But more than anything, he dreamed that Denese would one day experience the joy of being loved. But the morning's events had cast a dark shadow on those dreams, and he felt like any chances of them coming to pass as he had envisioned were gone. Even worse, he felt like his dream had become a nightmare. He had experienced a reversal of fates; he was no longer the hero but the victim of his own plot. Still worse, he realized that he had little to show for his efforts. After all this time, he had only been left with his present feelings of filth, confusion, fear, disappointment, and doubt.

This thought sprouted yet another emotion which was also not good. This emotion came from a place deep within his being, and rather quickly it began to boil over. This new emotion was the feeling of anger, and once it had fully consumed him, he was seething uncontrollably. His anger was mainly focused on the bridge and the reality that the happenings there had not turned out as he had desired. He was angry at himself for spending so much of his time and possessions in what now appeared to be a fruitless venture. He was also angry at the man in black for causing his dreams to unravel. Finally, he was angry at Denese for no other reason than just being herself, whether she was a hapless bridge dweller who couldn't help herself or a man-eating troll that had intentionally misled him.

Prior to leaving the Happy Land Hamburger, Brad had planned on returning home and busying himself with anything that he could find. But, with the arrival of his newfound anger, his plans had changed. An hour ago, the bridge would have been the last place on earth that he would have chosen to go. His natural inclination was to avoid the dangers that it posed him. But he was no longer thinking very clearly. His anger had clouded his judgment and washed away the fear that he had felt previously. Now he felt an overwhelming desire to be vindicated. He knew that this would only come through learning the truth, and if there was any truth to be had, it would have to come straight from the source. Therefore, he knew that he had to speak with Denese in person about these matters.

His anger fueled his efforts by pumping adrenaline into his veins. Instantly, he felt stronger and energized. Then the pain in his head and back went away. Filled with a new sense of determination, he began to vigorously pedal his bike toward the bridge. Along the way, he zoomed past the flock of crows still sitting in the trees. Immediately, their presence filled him with a sense of dread. He had hoped that they would have been gone by now. Because of their presence, a thought popped into his mind. He began to wonder if the man in black might still be lurking around. After cresting the next hill, he realized that his concerns were justified. The man in black had indeed not left. In fact, he was still leaning against the bridge sign smoking a cigarette.

At the sight of the man in black, Brad's courage began to waver. He began questioning his thoughts and motives. He realized that he had only been thinking about Denese. He hadn't considered that the man in black might still be around. Now he had a new dilemma. He had to get past him, but how he could accomplish this feat perplexed him, so he slowed his bike and brought it to a halt in the same spot as before.

Once again, the man in black stepped away from the sign and moved to the dead center of the road. For the next minute or so, he silently puffed on his cigarette. His eyes busily moved up and down as they studied Brad from head to toe. After he had finished smoking his cigarette, he tossed it to the ground, crushing it under his boot just as he had done before. His face had remained emotionless during this time, but before addressing Brad, he changed his countenance. To ease the tension in the air, he put on a sheepish grin.

"I can tell that you're upset, and you have a good reason for feeling this way. If I were you, I would feel exactly the same way. You know that you don't really deserve to feel like this. You didn't ask for any of this frustration. You were just trying to do a good deed and that is very commendable. But look where that got you. Your kindness was only trampled in the mud. No one likes to be taken for a fool. The truth is that this troll didn't deserve your kindness. If I were you, I wouldn't worry about her anymore. You deserve so much better than what she could offer anyway. Tell you what…I'd like to be your friend." At the mention of this suggestion, Brad's suspicion only increased all the more. "To demonstrate my sincerity, I would like to give you a gift. Now, this isn't just any gift. No, this is one of my most prized possessions. It was given to me by my father. It's very old and quite rare. In fact, you'll never find another like it. It is a truly amazing object, for it has the power to show you your future." Brad's eyes widened with curiosity over the man in black's last outlandish comment. "Yes, this object will allow you to see what others only dream about. It was made from pure magic, and whoever possesses it wields amazing power. I would like to give you this gift to demonstrate my sincerity."

He withdrew the object from one of his coat pockets and held it out for Brad to see. Brad immediately recognized the object as a hand mirror, and he could tell from its appearance that it was very old but in exquisite shape. The handle and surrounding rim appeared to be made of solid gold, and into the handle, he detected an ornamental inlay of some sort. Straining his eyes, he recognized that the design was the form of an angel. Then he peered into the mirror itself and immediately recognized his own reflection. As he continued looking into the mirror, he noticed that the image began to slowly change. His image faded and was replaced by a different one. He was still the person in the mirror, but his appearance had changed. He was much older. In fact, he was an adult. He was wearing different clothes. The setting was also different. He was no longer sitting upon his bicycle with the muddy road in the background. In this scene, he was dressed in a nice suit and standing in front of a very large crowd. He had been given an award of some sort. As he raised the award into the air, the people in the audience responded by leaping into a standing ovation.

While watching the scene unfold, he realized that he liked

what he saw. He had always dreamed of having a future such as this, but he never believed that it could come true. He would be the first to admit that thus far his life had been rather disappointing, and if the truth be told, he didn't see it changing. But the lack of opportunity hadn't stopped him from hoping for a better one. He dreamed of life free from his present struggles, and like the scene in the mirror, he also hoped that one day he might make his mark on this world. He wanted to leave his fingerprints behind, so that when he was gone, he would be remembered as a person who had made the world a better place.

As he continued to peer into the mirror, he realized that in some form or another his dreams had come to fruition. His life had amounted to something after all. Somehow, he had risen above his current circumstances and accomplished something of note. This revelation filled him with a sense of pride like he had never known. Then another sensation swept over him. It was one that he had never felt before. It was the feeling of power. Together, the combination of pride and power made him feel very good.

Watching himself in the mirror was an altogether surreal experience. Through the mirror, he was able to rise above his current place and transcend both time and space. He was no longer a helpless boy. Rather, he had become strong and capable. It was a new feeling for him, and he quickly discovered that it was a feeling that he rather enjoyed and wanted to last. However, deep down, he secretly feared that it wouldn't and then everything would have to return to the way it had been before. After feeling such power, he knew that it would be hard to return to his previous way of life. In this moment, he realized that he would be willing to do anything to keep this from happening. Since the mirror had been the source of his newfound sense of pride and power, he began to burn with a desire to possess it, and with every passing moment, this desire only increased.

Subconsciously, his body began leaning towards the mirror in an attempt to draw closer to it. As he stretched over the handlebars, his right foot slipped off the pedal. When this happened, he momentarily lost his balance and stumbled. Naturally, he took his eyes off the mirror and directed his gaze downward. While his eyes were diverted away, the sparkly red paint of his *Radio Flyer* bicycle caught his attention. In that instant, he experienced a flashback. He was taken back to the memory of his aunt's funeral and more specifically the time when he was alone with Mr. Johnson in the shed behind her house. He realized that he had once looked upon his bike in a very similar manner. He remembered how badly he had wanted this bike for his own. He had convinced himself that if he could just possess the bike that it would solve all of his problems. Later, he came to the painful realization that this had not been the case. His bike was only an object that was meant to be used and not worshiped. It had no magical powers in itself. Finally, he remembered Mr. Johnson's warning: "You are going to have to be especially careful. The world is a dangerous place, and it will lure you into all sorts of traps; traps that cause pain, suffering, and even death." Before looking back up, he paused to consider Mr. Johnson's advice in the context of his present situation. He had never trusted the man in black. He wondered why he would part with such a precious and powerful gift.

As he began considering the man in black's motives, he was struck by the possibility that this mirror might not really be a gift at all. Gifts were meant to be a blessing, but what if this object was not a blessing, but a curse? What if this object was one of the world's traps to which Mr. Johnson had alluded? What if he spent his remaining days staring into the image of his future and forgot to live life? This thought sent a chill down his spine, and immediately, he was put back on edge.

Quickly, he looked back up but carefully kept the mirror out of direct view. Instead, he focused his eyes on the man in black's face. He was taken aback by the man's ghastly appearance. In the time since he had last looked upon him, his face had undergone a transformation. His eyes had turned pitch black and were sunken into his skull. His skin had become pale and weathered looking, and his mouth carried a distorted grin which only served to expose a set of sharp, jagged teeth. Frightened, Brad jerked backwards. He was so startled that he almost fell off his bike, but at the last moment, he steadied himself. Once his balance had been regained, he looked back at the man in black, and this time, the image that he saw left him perplexed. In a millisecond, the man's appearance had changed back to normal. As far as he could tell, he looked exactly like he did when they had first met. He was in the process of pondering what all of this meant when the man in black interrupted his thoughts.

"Brad, I would like to give you this gift," and then he brought the mirror up to his face so that Brad would have to take another good look at it.

Instead, Brad quickly diverted his eyes to the side and said, "No thanks. I don't want it."

At the rejection of his offer, the man in black's countenance changed yet again. Except this time, it was not for the better. His face took on a look of scorn, and he began glaring at Brad through a pair of squinted eyes. He began clinching his teeth, making the muscles in his jaw bulge outwards. To Brad, there was a palpable feeling of hate in the air, and he knew that it was being directed solely at him. Finally, the man in black ended his silence and said in a rather harsh tone, "What are you doing here, boy?"

Rather timidly, Brad replied, "I just want to pass through, that's all."

"Didn't you hear what I said before or are you just stupid?"

"I heard you, but I still want to pass through."

"What are you trying to prove, boy? That you're brave? Hell, I'll give you that one. Now, just go on home."

"No, I need to speak to Denese."

"What don't you understand? This troll can't be trusted. You're only going to get yourself hurt."

"Well, that's a risk I'm willing to take. Stop worrying about me. Please, just let me pass."

The man in black erupted into laughter at Brad's last remark because it contained elements of both irony and truth. The irony was that he didn't care about Brad's well-being at all. In fact, the exact opposite was true. He wished that Brad was dead. However, there was an element of truth in his statement. The man in black had come because he was indeed worried. He was worried about the trouble that Brad would cause him if he continued on the same course. He didn't want him meddling with Denese. He wanted her to stay where she was. Thus, he had come to put Brad onto a different course, preferably one that had an actual dead end.

Since Brad wasn't changing his mind over the issue at hand, the man in black decided to change his tactics. "What do you think that you are going to accomplish? Do you really believe that you can be a friend to this troll?" After asking Brad this question, he remained silent for a minute or so. During this time, he slowly paced back and forth across the road, pretending to be in deep thought. After a few passes, he stopped abruptly as if he had experienced an epiphany. With folded arms, he turned and faced Brad. Then he moved his right hand up to his chin where he began to tap it ever so gently. All the while, he continued to behave as if he was contemplating some profound revelation. He finished his theatrical display by opening his eyes wide while making a gasping noise. Then he proceeded to speak again, "Ohh...ohh...I see what you're trying to do. You think that you can change this troll; that somehow you can make her better." While shaking his head and waving his finger in the air, the man in black continued, "That will never happen. You can't help her. In fact, you can't even help yourself. Don't you know what everybody has been saying about you? You're a pathetic loser. And they know about your family. They know that your father is a washed-up alcoholic and that your mother is helplessly depressed. You might as well give up because you will never help anybody, anytime, anywhere!"

Almost instantly, Brad's demeanor changed for the worse. His naturally dark-complexioned face turned pale as the color completely drained from his skin. His brown eyes became glossy as large tears began to coalesce in the corners. His posture also changed, becoming slightly hunched over as if a large weight had just been dropped onto his shoulders. Sniffling, he fought back the tears as best he could, but he couldn't contain them all, and a few tears spilled out and rolled down his cheeks. Using the back of his hand, he tried to discretely wipe them away, hoping to conceal the fact that the man in black had made him cry. But the man in black had indeed seen Brad's tears, and he began to smile at the sight of them, for it was in human suffering that he took his greatest pleasure. The sight of tears on Brad's face invigorated him, and like a shark smelling blood in the water, he became more aggressive with his attacks. Pretending to be a baby, he balled up his fist and started rubbing his eyes in a circular motion. Then he began chanting in a very sarcastic tone, "Go home little baby. Go home little baby." Having never faced such a blatant attack, Brad felt helpless. He had been completely demoralized. Then, feeling as if he had no other choice, he turned and went home as the man in black had suggested.

* * * *

The difference in his trip to and from the bridge was dramatic. On the way, he had powered down the road with great ease, but now the pedals on his bike felt frozen, forcing him to struggle mightily to make them turn. Expending the remainder of his energy, he forced his bike to move, but he quickly tired, and as a result, his bike just barely puttered down the road. On the way, he passed the crows once again, and like critics, they heckled him as he went by.

After what seemed like an eternity, Brad finally made it home. On a typical day, he would have washed off his bike prior to storing it in the garage, but today was not a typical day. In a rather uncharacteristic fashion, he drove his bike straight to the front door and quickly dismounted from it. Without any regard for his bike, he released his grip from the handlebars and walked away, letting it fall haphazardly to the ground. Once inside, he went directly to his room and slammed the bedroom door shut. With the remaining strength that he had left, he walked over to his bed and collapsed upon it. He reached for his favorite blanket, drawing it close to his face. He had hoped that in it he would find some comfort, but none was found because the man in black's words still echoed in his mind. His words were like flaming arrows that had been shot directly into his heart, and although there were no outward physical signs that he had been pierced, he still felt a deep ache in the center of his chest.

Previously, the man in black's words had left him feeling dirty, confused, and afraid, but after this last encounter, he began to experience a completely new set of emotions. He felt helpless and inadequate. He hated to admit it, but the man in black had been right. When he reflected over his life and its problems, he wondered what he had been thinking. How could he help anyone? He couldn't even help himself. He was a complete and utter wreck. He wasn't special in any way, shape, or form. He was just a tiny speck among the sea of other specks that covered the face of earth. In that moment, he realized that he was indeed quite insignificant. This revelation brought back the question of what was his purpose for existing. For it, he did not have an answer, and so he remained feeling very helpless, inadequate, and insignificant. As he lay in bed, large tears began to flow from his big brown eyes. It was in this moment that he began to lose all hope, and his spirit began sinking back down into the miry muck of depression.

His present condition reminded him of his first trip to the bridge. On that day, he had been in the throes of a deep and dark depression. He distinctly remembered the feeling of hopelessness that filled him as he read the sign "Bridge Closed–Dead End." If not for the sign, he probably would not have gone any further down the road, but at that moment, he felt like the sign had only confirmed what he must do. He realized that he no longer wanted any part of this miserable existence. He had indeed reached the end of himself, and he saw little reason for continuing onward if this was all that life had to offer. Thus, he had come to the bridge expecting to find death, but in a mysteriously miraculous way, he had been delivered from this fate. He had been unconscious during the whole ordeal, so the events surrounding this time were uncertain. After conducting his own investigation, he had come to the conclusion that he had been saved by Denese, and it wasn't until he had met the man in black that he had any reason to believe otherwise. In his heart, he still believed in Denese, but those convictions weren't as strong as they once had been. In fact, he would be lying if he said that he didn't have at least a few doubts. To remedy this situation, he had attempted to visit Denese, but once again, he had been ambushed by the man in black.

After his first encounter with the man in black, he returned home with questions about Denese, but after this most recent encounter, he had left with questions about himself. He had been forced to take a long, hard look at who he really was. During this time of introspection, he could no longer ignore his faults. He realized that he had only been deceiving himself because the self-image that he had been portraying was not who he really was. It was only something that he had conceived in his mind. His true identity was, in reality, something quite different. This was hard for him to accept, but he knew that it was true. He realized that he didn't need the man in black's mirror to distort his perception of reality. He had been doing a very good job of that on his own. Like the mirror, he had only been filling his mind with what he wanted to see. At the present, this translated into the belief that he was something special, but when he looked at his life, he knew that this was far from being true. In the future, he hoped that he would one day be successful. He dreamed that he would make a difference in the lives of others. When he looked into the man in black's mirror, this is what he saw. Sadly, he knew that if he looked into a real mirror that he wouldn't find any evidence that this person existed. He hated to admit it, but the man in black had been right. He couldn't help anyone. He couldn't even help himself. He was just a poor, broken, little boy who lived in an old, broken, little home.

NINE

While lying in bed, an idea popped into his head, and because of its ridiculous nature, he dismissed it altogether. But this idea kept sneaking back into his thoughts, and so he began to actually consider it. Once again, he concluded that it was too crazy, so he tried pushing it out of his mind for good. Several minutes later, he let out a moan and covered his head with a pillow because he realized that this thought wasn't going to go away. It was an altogether crazy idea. The thought of returning to the bridge sent shivers down his spine. On this day, the bridge had only brought him pain, sadness, and fear for his life. However, as he continued to ponder the idea, he was reminded of his first trip to the bridge. On that day, he had also felt great pain. At the hands of his father, he had fallen victim to the ruthless clutches of depression, and it had forced him to run. In the process, he had stumbled upon the bridge. As he thought over his first encounter there, he realized that the bridge had not caused his feelings, but somehow in a rather curious manner, it had helped him deal with those feelings. As he reflected over the weeks that followed, he saw how his depression had slowly improved, and then at some unknown point, it had just disappeared. Until this moment, he had not recognized that his depression had indeed faded. He just knew that he had been feeling better, but as to why, he hadn't really been concerned. But now that his depression had returned in full force, he realized that it had been gone, albeit for a short period of time.

Speculating about his future, he wondered if another visit to the bridge might actually bring further healing. He could only hope that this might be the case. However, he suspected that the man in black was probably still there, and the mere thought of him filled his heart with shear dread. The man in black was the reason that his depression had returned. He had successfully prevented him from going to the bridge on the last two occasions. Therefore, he reckoned that his next trip to the bridge would likely be no different. He had only met the man in black twice but that was enough. He searched his mind, attempting to find another way out of the depression that held him captive, but after a few minutes, he realized that there was no other way. He had no other options. To find healing, his path would have to intersect with the bridge once again. He knew that this wouldn't be any easy path because it was going to force him to face his fears head on.

In this moment, Brad understood for the very first time that his life had become inexplicably bound to the bridge. It began on the first, fateful day when he had been drawn to its old dilapidated structure. Over the weeks that followed, it continued drawing him to its doorstep. It had brought him healing once, and so he believed that it could possibly bring him healing a second time. His desire to visit the bridge had transcended a want. It had become a need. In his whole life, he had never experienced such a mixture of emotions. On one hand, he truly needed the bridge and had to go, yet on the other hand, he also felt a terrible aversion for it and wanted to stay away. His decision had come down to a battle between his heart and mind. His heart tugged him onward, whereas his mind beckoned him to stay. In the end, his heart was the victor.

As soon as the decision was made, he got out of bed. His body began aching with even the slightest movements. He briefly considered lying back down and waiting until tomorrow, but he realized that compared to how he felt physically he was more tired of how he felt mentally. More than anything, he wanted to be free from his depression, and he knew that staying in bed wouldn't move him any closer to his goal. Thus, he continued onward.

As expected, he found the man in black at the same location as before, except this time, he wasn't leaning against the sign or smoking a cigarette. He was already standing in the middle of the road with his arms folded across his body. From his posture, Brad immediately sensed that the man in black meant business—he carried a look of seriousness that he had not seen before. For fear of getting too close, Brad stopped his bike even further back and simply waited for the man in black to make his move as he had come with no plan of his own. He knew that he needed to get past the man in black, but as to how this was going to transpire, he had not a clue.

On this encounter, the man in black didn't waste any time on theatrics or words. He spoke to the point using a voice that reflected the anger that shone on his face. "I tried playing nice, but you just didn't get it. In fact, I even gave you two chances. But this is your third strike and that means you're out. You thought that you felt bad before, but now I'm going to give you something that will make you feel really bad." While uttering this threat, the man in black clinched his hands into a fist, and then he began walking towards Brad. Overwhelmed with terror, Brad froze like a deer in headlights. He had a moment of déjà vu. The image of his father approaching him with a hot poker flashed into his mind. Out of instinct, he turned his bike and began peddling as fast as his legs would go. Behind him, the man in black broke into a run as he continued his pursuit, but he gave up when he realized that he couldn't catch him. As the gap widened between them, Brad heard the man in black yelling in the background,

"You can run but you cannot hide. There is no place on earth that you can go where I won't find you. This isn't over, Brad Buerger! No, it's far from being over!" Then the man in black broke into evil, bloodcurdling laugh.

Motivated out of sheer fright, Brad pressed onward, peddling frantically the whole way home. Once in the front yard, he leaped from his bike and ran to his room, slamming and locking every door on the way. So terrific was his fright that he chose to crawl not under the covers but the bed itself, hiding like a mouse. For several hours, he remained this way and did not move away from underneath the bed until he heard his mother return from work.

Brad desperately wanted to tell his mother about the man in black, but from her countenance, he knew that this was not the time. Within a few minutes of returning home, she had retired to her room for the night. Feeling safer in his room, Brad decided to do the same. While lying in his bed, he noticed that his body had begun aching from head to toe. Reflecting over the day and his trips to and from the bridge, he realized that it had indeed been a very long and eventful day. He was exhausted, and his mind was only telling him what his body already knew. Rolling onto his side, he let out a big yawn, and within a few minutes, he was sound asleep.

* * * *

The following day was Sunday, and the atmosphere at the Buergers' home was unusually quiet. On Sundays, Mrs. Buerger didn't have to work, and so she always slept late. Around ten-thirty, she finally began to stir. As she made her coffee and settled into her morning routine, she failed to notice that Brad hadn't left his room. For the next couple of hours, she lounged around the house, reading the newspaper and watching TV. She hadn't been concerned about Brad. She figured that he was just outside playing. However, when he didn't show up for lunch, she began looking for him. At this point, she realized that the door to his room was closed. She knocked on his bedroom door and called out his name. When there was no response, she attempted to open the door but discovered that it was locked. She knocked louder. When there was no response a second time, she grew panicked. She ran back to the kitchen and began fumbling through the drawers, searching for the master key to the bedrooms. In her mind, she envisioned the worst, and this thought only fueled her frantic behavior. After tearing apart most of the kitchen, she finally found the key. Then she sprinted back to his bedroom, inserted it into the keyhole, and forcefully flung the door open.

Preparing herself for the worst, she cautiously stepped into his room. After a quick scan, she discovered that Brad was lying in his bed. The sight of his body brought forth feelings of both relief and concern. She felt relief at finding him, but she also felt extremely concerned because he had not responded to her calling. She quickly moved to his side. When she saw that his cheeks were flushed, she breathed a sigh of relief that he was alive. Kneeling at his bed, she gently placed her hand on his forehead. He was burning hot with fever. She pulled back the covers. His pajamas were drenched with sweat. Her concern began to build again. She called out to Brad, but when he didn't respond, she began to gently shake him, trying to rouse him. He responded with a weak moan but never gained consciousness. Mrs. Buerger ran back to the kitchen and dialed 911. In short order, the paramedics arrived, and after a brief evaluation, they rushed him off to the hospital.

* * * *

A few days later when Brad regained consciousness, he experienced déjà vu for the second time in under a week. He found that he was lying in another hospital bed. He had just been in the hospital a few months earlier. However, on this occasion, there was one notable difference. When he awoke this time, he found his mother sitting by his bedside. Her presence instantly warmed his heart. During his previous stay in hospital, he had awakened to an empty and lonely hospital room, and sadly, it had remained this way up to the day of his discharge. But from start to finish, this hospital visit was altogether different. From the very moment that he awoke, his mother demonstrated a form of love that he never knew existed. She showered him with hugs and kisses and constantly pampered him. She went out of her way to make sure that he was comfortable and had the things that he needed. On one occasion, she left to get him some ice cream, and while she was gone, he learned from the nursing staff that she had remained by his bedside the entire time that he had been unconscious. She often sang to him as she held and caressed his hands. Finally before leaving, the nurse also told him that she frequently found his mother sobbing at his bedside.

Toward the end of his hospitalization, he witnessed some of his mother's tears. While at his bedside, she broke down and explained that she thought that she had lost him. Then she went on to explain that something had moved inside her heart when she had found him lying unconscious. She realized that she had failed to be the mother that she was supposed to be. She had allowed circumstances in her life to cloud her vision, but this was no longer the case. She was seeing clearly now and knew what was truly important. With tear-stained eyes, she begged him for forgiveness. Then she made him a promise that she was going to change for the better.

Brad could have never envisioned that his illness would have achieved such an outcome. Prior to his hospitalization, his relationship with his mother had suffered from its own form of sickness. In fact, their relationship had been at death's door, but his sickness had miraculously brought their relationship back to life. In a million years, he could have never imagined such an outcome.

His recovery was just as miraculous. Within a few days of waking, the doctors had determined that he could go home. In the end, their final assessment was that he had contracted a very serious infection known as the West Nile virus. Once in the bloodstream, the virus would attack the host's brain and spinal cord, and it could lead to high fevers, confusion, coma and even death. The virus was transmitted from birds to humans by mosquitoes. There had been an outbreak of the West Nile virus in the Happyville community. The doctors weren't exactly sure why this outbreak had occurred, but many of them had attributed the spread of this illness to a large flock of crows that had recently inhabited the area.

One week after being admitted to the hospital, Brad was discharged. It was a joyous occasion. Brad did have some apprehension about returning home because he feared that his mother would revert to her old ways, but his fears were quickly alleviated because he found that his mother had remained true to her word. She had made a commitment to change, and she wasn't going to be deterred. For starters, she decided to cut back to part time at the Cup of Fun Coffee House so that she could spend more time at home. Before leaving in the morning, she would cook him breakfast and then see him off to school. In the evening, they would sit and share dinner together. Once the meal was done and the kitchen cleaned, she would help him with his homework. At bedtime, she would kiss him on the forehead and wish him a good night.

Admittedly, Brad enjoyed the attention and more specifically the love that his renewed relationship with his mother had brought him. Secretly, he had longed for her love, and now that he was receiving it regularly, his broken heart was beginning to mend. He also noticed that he was beginning to climb out of the pit of his depression. His body had also begun to heal from the infection that had recently ravaged it. Overall, he felt the best that he had in quite a long time. Life at home was good, and his life at school was also going well. For reasons that he couldn't explain, his teachers and fellow students were demonstrating a form of kindness that they had never before displayed. From beginning to end, his days were far better than anything he could have imagined.

* * * *

Despite all that was going so right in his world, there was a new area in his life where he had begun to struggle. This new area had to deal with the issue of sleep. Since returning home from the hospital, he had started suffering with nightmares. Each night, he would wake up terrified, gasping for breath and covered in a cold sweat. Because of his nightmares, he had developed some anxiety over bedtime because it brought him to the very doorstep of the thing that he feared the most, namely the man in black. From night to night, his nightmares would differ, but there was always one constant about his nightmares and that was the man in black. No matter where he went, the man in black was always searching and chasing after him. He knew that the man in black's sole purpose for seeking him was because he wanted to do both his body and soul harm. Each night, Brad would wake up just as he was about to be overtaken by the man in black. From one night to the next, the context of his nightmare might differ, but the ending never changed. He was always being relentlessly pursued by an evil that wanted nothing more than to see him destroyed. The last time that he had seen the man in black, he had shouted at him, "You can run but you cannot hide. There is no place on earth that you can go where I won't find you." At the conclusion of each nightmare, he would awaken with these words ringing in his ears.

During the day, he would try to forget about the man in black, but what he discovered was that he truly couldn't run from him. Everywhere he turned, he saw constant reminders of his existence. Largely, these reminders came in the form of the flock of black crows that had come to reside in the area. Their arrival had directly corresponded with the man in black's arrival, and ever since that fateful day on the road leading to the bridge, he had come to associate the presence of crows with the presence of the man in black himself. Regardless of where he went in town, they were there. In the morning, they were outside his home. When he left school, they were there as well. Wherever he went, they followed, and their constant presence in his life served as a continual reminder of the man in black.

He had already faced a number of adversaries in his young life, but to date, he had never faced a nemesis quite like this. Mysteriously, the man in black's presence had begun to haunt him even when he wasn't visibly present. In fact, it had been almost two weeks since their last encounter, yet somehow he was still reaching out and affecting him through his thoughts and dreams. He was at a loss as to what to do. He tried to shoo away the crows, but they didn't fear him. He thought about boarding himself up inside his home, but logistically, he knew that this wouldn't work. To keep himself from having nightmares, he had tried to stay awake at night, but his attempts always failed. At some point, he would inevitably drift off to sleep, and then the nightmares would quickly follow. In the end, he discovered that he fallen into yet another vicious cycle that he didn't know how to break.

As time progressed, he found that this cycle had caused his body to wear down. The combination of anxiety, paranoia, and lack of sleep had begun taking its toll on a body that had already been weakened by a recent illness. In regards to his illness, he had begun to suspect that the man in black might have also had a hand in it as well. The barrage of attacks had left him quite shaken. In the hospital, he had grown stronger, but since coming home, he had been getting steadily weaker. His anxiety and paranoia had put him in a state of perpetual fear. The newfound joy that he had experienced at home and school turned out to be short-lived. The glow that had temporarily lit up his face disappeared as well. In their place, he became more reclusive, spending ever increasing amounts of time alone in his bedroom. His mother had noted the marked change in his demeanor and inquired about it. Brad didn't know how to tell his mother about the bridge, Denese, or the man in black, so he kept silent about the true cause of his affliction. Fearing that his illness had returned, his mother did what any good mother would do. She called the doctor and made him an appointment for the very next day.

* * * *

After awakening from another restless night, Brad climbed out of bed and began his daily routine of dressing himself. While dressing, he had the vague recollection that his mother had intended to take him to the doctor, and this thought made his stomach twist tightly in knots. He had never fancied going to the doctor, and given the recent events in his life, he had started liking them even less. He had seen far too many over the last few months for his taste. He knew that their intentions were good as they were merely trying to help, and for this, he was very grateful because without their help he probably wouldn't be alive. They had successfully saved his life not just once but twice. Despite this fact, he still had a great deal of apprehension about visiting them. He had always been afraid of doctors. It wasn't that he didn't like them as people. Rather, he didn't like what they could do to him. He was terrified of needles, and all of the poking that he had received recently hadn't helped with this fear.

While brushing his teeth, he had a brief moment of hope

that his memory of going to the doctor had only been another bad dream. When his mother stepped in to give him a reminder, his hopes were quickly dashed. After finishing up in the bathroom, he joined her in the kitchen where he found breakfast prepared. Once breakfast was over, she packed him into the car, and together, they headed for their family doctor.

At the doctor's office, he found that the waiting room was packed full of people, ranging widely in ages. Some of them were obviously sick as they intermittently sniffled and coughed, whereas others appeared to be completely healthy. A number of them were reading magazines to pass the time. A few of the smaller children were on the floor playing with toys while their mothers were busily chatting away on cell phones. Finally, there was an old man in the corner who had managed to somehow fall asleep, and to the amusement of everyone else, he would occasionally rip off a loud snort.

For the better part of an hour, they waited, and for this period of waiting, Brad was glad. He preferred waiting in lieu of having to see the doctor. As time passed, he began to secretly hope that the doctor had been called away to the hospital to tend to an emergency, and because he couldn't be in two places at once, his appointment would have to be canceled. However, his hopes were broken into pieces when he heard his name called aloud. With his apprehension surging, he and his mother followed the nurse to one of the examining rooms. After taking his vital signs, the nurse left, shutting the door on the way out. As a whole, the examining room was cold and drab. There was very little that he could do to pass the time. In many ways, he felt like a caged animal because he only wanted to be freed from this place. As he sat, he kept a watchful eye on the door. At one point, he thought that he saw the doorknob turning. Flooded with fear, he almost jumped out of his seat.

Realizing that his nerves were getting the better of him, he got up and began pacing around the room. On the far side of the examining room, he found something of interest. It was a stack of pamphlets. At first, he expected that these little pamphlets would only contain literature about various health-related topics, but after a quick glance, he wasn't so sure that they were health-related at all. There were two different stacks. One pamphlet was black, and it had the word "CrossRoads" written across the front cover. The other pamphlet was brightly colored with pinks, yellows, and greens, and it was entitled "The Forgotten Easter." Of the two, his eyes had been drawn to the brightly colored stack of pamphlets. Reaching out, he picked up one and began thumbing through it. Meanwhile, his mother had left her seat and joined him. Unlike Brad, she had been mysteriously drawn to the black pamphlet. Curious about its content, she picked one up and began to examine it. They both quickly discovered that inside the cover of these little booklets there was a story, and after reading the first few lines, they realized that they weren't medically-related. Curious about their contents, they returned to their seats and continued reading.

TEN

The Forgotten Easter

"Peter...Peter Rabbit...it's time to wake up." And then suddenly Peter heard the old familiar sound of his mother's voice ringing throughout the briar patch as her words settled in his long, slender ears. Like antennas, his ears began twitching, positioning themselves in order to get the best reception. Realizing that his mother had beckoned him to awaken from his slumber, Peter began slowly stirring. First, he rubbed his eyes, and then he let out a big yawn. After he had finished stretching his legs, he began to venture forth from the warmth of his bedding spot to join his mother and father at the edge of the briar patch. Upon seeing him, his mother said, "Good morning, Peter."

"Good morning, Momma," replied Peter with a smile.

"I am starving. I can't wait for breakfast. How about you Peter?" his father asked.

"Me too, Daddy. Let's go. I'll race you." Before his father could reply, little Peter was bounding up the hill heading for the grassy meadow where they usually ate. His mother and father chuckled at their son's youthful exuberance, and then they too followed suit, hopping up the hill after him. At the top of the hill, Peter stopped dead in his tracks. Concerned by his sudden change in demeanor, his parents sped up their pace and quickly joined him atop the hill. Together, they sat staring out across the grassy meadow observing the commotion taking place before them. For several minutes, they remained silent as they studied the scene. Out of curiosity, other animals began to slowly emerge from the woods and join the Rabbit family on the edge of the meadow.

From their vantage point, they saw humans, both large and small. The children were scurrying around the meadow in a frenetic and what seemed to be a haphazard manner. Every few steps, they would stop and pick up a brightly colored egg, toss it into a basket, and then they would start off in a different direction, repeating the process all over again. Meanwhile, their parents stood off to the side where they laughed, smiled, and pointed at their children. Little Peter was the first to break the silence that had developed among the woodland creatures. "Momma, what are the humans doing?" he asked.

"They are collecting what humans call Easter eggs." To this, a questioning look broke across Peter's face. She continued, "Easter eggs are chicken eggs that have been colorfully painted."

Probing deeper, Peter asked, "Momma, who put the Easter eggs there?"

"Their parents secretly placed them in the meadow, but they tell their children that the Easter bunny left them."

"The Easter bunny...that's silly...everyone knows that bunnies don't lay eggs," replied Peter.

"I know, honey. It is silly. But that's how humans celebrate Easter."

"Momma, what is Easter?" asked Peter.

"Oh...now that is a good question, but I'm afraid that it's not one that can be quickly answered." Then Peter's mother took her eyes off of her son and gazed back at the humans frolicking on the meadow. As she watched them, her countenance became one of great sadness. Then she closed her eyes and took in a deep breath. When she finally opened her eyes again, she turned them back to Peter and said, "Well, I guess you're old enough to learn the true meaning of Easter. Everyone gather around. You all need to hear this." The animals followed her command and nestled down near her, forming a semicircle in the grass. Once all the creatures were settled, she began again. "Many, many ages ago, animals and man were friends." There was a murmur of disbelief that arose from the crowd that Mother Rabbit let die down before proceeding again. "Yes, it is true. At the dawn of the age during the time of Eden, animals and man once lived together in harmony. They worked side by side. They conversed, ate, laughed and cried together. Both animal and man were ruled by one who was neither man nor animal. It is said that he was present before anything was and that he was the source of all creation. And this creator ruled as a kind and loving king, and all who lived in his kingdom were truly blessed. It was a time of unparalleled joy."

Questions like "What happened?" "Why don't we live in peace anymore?" and "Where is this king?" began to rumble up from within the crowd.

Once the animals quieted down, Mother Rabbit began again. "There was another...one who was also neither man nor animal. He was second in command and answered only to the king. But he let his pride destroy him. He became jealous of the king and coveted his power. His desire consumed him, and ultimately he betrayed the king. He took the form of a snake and misled the first man, a man named Adam, into believing that he was smarter than the king. In doing so, Adam also betrayed the king. On that day, man fell from the king's good grace, and sadly, he took all of the animals with him. Both man and animal were banished from the kingdom and a curse was placed upon the earth. Man has been at war with all of creation ever since. They quickly lost the ability to communicate with animals, and for a very long time, they lost the ability to communicate with their king."

"Momma, what happened to the snake?" asked Peter.

"He still exists today. He roams the earth taking any form that suits him. You know him primarily as the black wolf." Peter's eyes grew large, and he slunk back into his seat at the mention of the name wolf. The other animals had a similar reaction to hearing that name. Mother Rabbit began again, "Yes, after all of these years, he is still bent on killing, stealing, and destroying all that the king has made."

Squirrel had nervously been nibbling on a nut but stopped his chewing and asked, "What happened next?"

"Let's see…where was I? Oh, yes…for many ages, it continued in this manner. Man and animal were separated from their creator king. Together, they lived on earth suffering terribly. They died in darkness, having forgotten their true origins and their king who had created them. But from a far away land, the king continued to watch as they struggled to find the way to truth and life. As he watched them struggle, his heart broke because he loved them deeply. In fact, the truth is that he had never stopped loving them. Ultimately, the pain that filled his heart became so great that it drove him to do something truly unimaginable. In a single act of self-sacrifice, he reversed the curse that had been placed on the earth. In doing so, he gave both man and animal a second chance to be in relationship with him."

"Hee...haw…hee…haw…how did he do that?" asked donkey.

"One day, a beautiful little lamb mysteriously appeared in these very woods. He was a kind, gentle, and humble little lamb, and he spoke only truth. He told the animals of things that they had long forgotten. He reminded them of their creator king. He told them that the king still loved them and wanted to be in a relationship with them again. Many of the animals believed the lamb, and in their believing, they became filled with a hope like they had never known before. Wolf was ruling over these woods at that time, and he became extremely angry that the lamb had reminded the people about their creator king since he had tried so very hard to make everyone forget about him. To suppress the truth from spreading, wolf had the lamb killed." Upon hearing this startling ending, all the animals covered their mouths and let out a gasp. "But something happened that the wolf hadn't anticipated. When the wolf killed the innocent lamb, he released a hidden power that had been created prior to our world's beginning, and this power brought the lamb back to life." After hearing this good news, the animals began clapping and cheering in unison. "But he didn't come back as a lamb. No, he returned as a king…a lion king. The animals hadn't realized that the creator king had returned to their world as a lamb in order to sacrifice himself so that all who believed in him could come and be with him in his new kingdom."

"B-b-but what about the h-h-humans?" stuttered beaver.

"At the same time that the lamb appeared to the animals, a man appeared to the humans. Like the lamb, he came teaching the truth, and like the lamb, the wolf killed him. They nailed him to a tree. But he didn't stay dead either. He arose from the dead. Then he revealed that he was the creator king in disguise. The humans call this man Jesus, and like the lamb, he came to sacrifice himself so that all who believed in him could come and be with him in his new kingdom."

"Why do the humans call it Easter?" squeaked mouse.

"After Jesus came back to life and before he returned to his kingdom, he told the humans that he would forgive them of their sins if they would only ask. No sin was too great. He would remove every one as far as the east is from the west. That is why they call it East-er," replied Mother Rabbit.

"Why do the humans collect Easter eggs?" clucked chicken. "I mean…what does that have to do with Jesus?"

Mother Rabbit turned and looked at the humans on the meadow. The children were scampering around in blissful ignorance. Her countenance took the appearance of sadness once again. "It has nothing to do with Jesus or the real meaning of Easter," said Mother Rabbit. "It is just another scheme of the black wolf. He doesn't want any of the humans to remember what Jesus did for them. He has brainwashed them into believing Easter is about bunnies, eggs, and candy."

"That's terrible," yelled deer.

"Momma, we have to do something. We can't leave them like this," said Peter.

"I have an idea," announced owl. "Who…who…who is with me?" All the animals raised either a paw or wing. "OK, this is what we are going to do."

In short order, the animals finished their assignments. The project was complete, but there was one final thing that had to be done. It was something that would require a great deal of courage, and when owl asked for a volunteer from the group, brave little Peter was the only one to step forward. He kissed his mother and hugged his father and then hopped out into the meadow. It was a good distance to the humans, but he traversed it quickly. When he was within a few feet of the children, he stopped and waited. Before long, he was noticed. Upon seeing a real Easter bunny, the children became very excited and created quite a commotion. They wanted to hold little Peter in their arms. But each time that they neared him, he would hop a few feet away. He kept this up until he had led them back to where the animals had been gathered, and then he hopped away quickly and hid in the woods.

Then the children stopped on the grassy knoll, gazing curiously at what stood before them. Soon their parents joined them, and together they stood in silence studying the object erected at the edge of the meadow. The youngest of the children broke the silence by asking, "Daddy, what is it?"

"I don't know. I have never seen anything like it before," replied her father.

Then one of the other parents spoke, "I have seen one of these before. But it was a long time ago. When my grandfather was still alive, he used to speak of it often. It is called a cross."

"What does it mean?" asked the child.

"I am trying to remember. Oh, yes…it's starting to come back to me now. It's a story of hope and new beginnings."

"Please tell us the story," the children begged.

The man grinned and told the children to have a seat. He had forgotten the message of the cross, but in an instant it had been renewed in his heart and mind, and the joy that it had brought him as a child was once again his.

* * * *

I hope that you enjoyed this story. But there is one thing that you should know; this was no story at all. The events told were true. Two thousand years ago, Jesus came and walked on this earth. He came bearing a message of great hope. And his message was that through his death on the cross, we could all be reconciled to him. If we would only turn to him, we could have a new beginning here on earth, and we would be counted as heirs in his kingdom. For Jesus said, "*There are many rooms in my house, I would not tell you this if it were not true. I am going there to prepare a place for you. After I go and prepare a place for you. I will come back and take you to be with me so that you may be where I am*" (John 14:2-3 NCV). Please consider the following question carefully. If you died today, would you be known and received by Jesus into his kingdom? If you don't have a personal relationship with him, then I invite you to begin one with him now.

ELEVEN

CrossRoads

Right on schedule, the sun broke over the horizon, signaling the beginning of a new day in a part of the world known as Happyville. A few minutes later, alarm clocks began chirping, buzzing, and beeping across the city while its inhabitants responded by stirring from their slumber. Thousands stretched and yawned as they arose from their beds to begin their normal routine of brushing teeth, dressing, combing hair, and eating breakfast. Then with breakfast only halfway to their bellies, the mad dash of the day began, and just like marbles being poured onto the floor, everyone scattered into different directions as they made their way to their desired destination. From the surface, it was just another day, not much different than any other. But for two individuals, this day would be quite unlike any other.

* * * *

For a moment in time, all the eyes in heaven turned towards the intersection of Jesse Jewell and EE Butler Parkway. Their attention had been drawn to this crossroads because in a few seconds an event of eternal proportions was about to occur.

From above, a white Honda minivan could be seen traveling southbound on EE Butler Parkway. It was moving methodically in the left-hand lane toward Jesse Jewell Parkway. At the same time a black BMW convertible could be seen racing in and out of traffic on Jesse Jewell Parkway. It was rapidly approaching the intersection with EE Butler Parkway. Just ahead the light had turned yellow but rather than brake, the black BMW accelerated, but before it reached the intersection, the light turned red. Realizing that it was too late to stop, the BMW continued onward. On EE Butler Parkway, the light had just turned green, and the white minivan which had been coasting towards the intersection began to accelerate through it. Just before impact, the drivers of both vehicles had a moment of lucidity as they realized the gravity of their predicament. In this moment, visions of their life's work passed through their mind. All of their successes and failures, joys and sorrows, dreams and regrets flashed before them. Then in an instant, those visions disappeared as the reality of their current situation returned. Time sped back up and with it came the inevitable collision of the black BMW with the white minivan. They smashed into each other at the crossroads, creating a mass of smoking, hot metal. The end result of this meeting was that on this day two people died.

* * * *

Twenty minutes earlier…

The driver of the white minivan

"I know you are at work, but I was hoping that I could talk to you for a minute. You won't believe what just happened to me. I just checked my voicemail. I don't know how I missed it, but the clinic called yesterday. I got the job…I got the job! Can you believe it!!! It is such an answer to prayer. I hate to say it, but I was beginning to wonder if God was listening to me at all. I was starting to lose hope, but he has provided for us yet again. God is good all the time. He has never let us down. I am going to head over there to fill out some paperwork after I drop off the kids at school. Maybe we can finally get the air conditioning in the minivan fixed. Anyway, I hope that you have a great day, honey. I will see you at church tonight…Bye."

* * * *

The driver of the black BMW

"Hello…What? I don't believe this!!! I told him earlier in week to finish this deal. His mistake is going to cost me a fortune. How could he do this to me??? He is going to pay for this… Yes, I know that his wife is ill and that he has been extremely busy caring for his two small children. That's not my fault. I am jumping in my BMW right now and coming down there. When I get there, I am going to make an example of him to the whole company by tossing him out on the street."

* * * *

The present…

As the drivers of both vehicles breathed their last breath, their souls separated from their physical bodies and drifted through the very fabric of time and space to enter a place known as the judgment seat. Unfortunately, their experiences were quite different.

The driver of the white minivan

Peering through squinted eyes, Amy slowly opened her eyes as she waited for them to accommodate to the blinding light that surrounded her. After her vision had been restored, she was able to take in her surroundings, and the image that she saw took her breath away. She quickly realized that she had never seen so much beauty in all of her life. The room was expansive with tall, towering ceilings that appeared to be made of glass, and above it, she saw what seemed like a thousand galaxies. The walls of the room were covered with a magnificent purple fabric, and pristine marble colonnades lined the walls at regular intervals. The floor of the room was a calm, clear sheet of water. The source of the light within the room wasn't easily recognizable, but Amy thought to herself that regardless of its origin, it was the purest and most vibrant light that she had ever seen.

From the far reaches of the room, she turned her focus upon herself. At this point, she realized that her body was clothed with a majestic white robe and that her head had been adorned with a beautiful golden crown, layered in fine jewels. Next, her eyes moved to the place where she was sitting, and then she realized that she was resting upon a large golden throne. She was examining the engravings on the throne when she was startled by a voice in the distance.

"Hello, Amy," the voice said.

Amy looked up in an attempt to identify the voice's source. Walking toward her was a man. He had long, flowing, brown hair and a well-kept beard. His eyes flickered like the light of a candle. He was dressed in an unblemished white robe, and beside him walked a large powerful lion and a small frail lamb. As they walked on the floor of water, ripples spread out across the room. She was overwhelmed by a warm, tingling sensation of love. It covered her from head to toe and reached the deep recesses of her soul. It was like nothing that she had ever felt before, and she knew instantly that she never wanted to be without it again. Her mind told her that the origin of such love could only come from one source. Thus, she was certain that she was in presence of Jesus. She desperately wanted to run to him and clutch his neck and bury her face into his chest. But she felt herself being restrained by some supernatural power.

"Jesus, where am I?" Amy questioned.

"You are on the judgment seat," Jesus responded. Immediately, fear began rising up from within her as thoughts like "Was I good enough?" or "Will he want me?" raced through her mind. "Fear not, my child. Your name has been written in the Book of Life for quite some time now."

With a look of confusion on her face, Amy asked, "So why am I being judged?"

"In order to receive your due reward for services rendered in the name of the Kingdom. Now come to me good and faithful servant. In you, I am well pleased."

Amy sprung from her seat and bounded across the watery floor. Jesus stood smiling with open arms, and she fell into them. After their embrace, she gazed deeply into his eyes as he gently caressed her cheek with his fingers. But she noticed something missing as she took in the beauty of his face.

"Jesus, where is your crown?"

"Oh, my precious child, you are wearing it. You are going to sit with me on my throne. Now come with me. Since you are finally home, it is time to meet the rest of your family."

As Jesus said these words, the room began overflowing with men, women, and children. Many of them she knew from her past. As she walked through the crowd, she was met with warm smiles, loving embraces, and sweet kisses.

To Amy, it was truly a homecoming for the ages.

* * * *

The driver of the black BMW

Mike strained his eyes in hopes of seeing anything. But despite his best efforts, he realized that any further attempts would be in vain as he was surrounded by a pitch-black darkness. Accompanying this overwhelming darkness was a sensation of bone-chilling cold. In an attempt to warm his body, he began rubbing his arms with his hands. It was at this point that he realized that he was completely naked. Like an overflowing spring, fear began to well up from within.

Panicked, Mike began yelling, "Help…Help…Somebody help me, please!!!"

"Yes, Mike," a voice responded.

"Who's there and how do you know my name?" Mike asked timidly.

"It is I. I am here," the voice replied.

Mike searched the recesses of his mind in an attempt to locate that voice from his databank. But his searching came up empty. Then he was struck with the sudden realization that he was being confronted by God.

"G-G-God is that you?" Mike asked.

"Yes, Mike, it is I," responded God.

"God, why is it so dark in here?"

"Mike, I have chosen darkness for you because I thought that is what you would desire."

"What do you mean?"

"Your entire existence was spent in darkness, so I naturally assumed that you would be more comfortable in the dark."

"I don't understand."

"You chose to spend your life on earth apart from me, living out your own selfish desires. You chose to avoid the light of my truth and stay in the darkness of your world."

"When did you ever come to me? I am quite sure that I would have followed you, but I don't remember you coming."

"Mike, I have been with you since the day that you were conceived. I formed you in your mother's womb. I was there the day that you were born into the world. I watched you grow. I picked you up when you fell and healed your scrapes. It was I who lay with you at night when you slept. I was there when you succeeded and were happy. I was there when you failed and were sad. I protected you from evils that you never knew existed. I blessed you with so very much…wealth, health, family, and honor. Through the years, I whispered in your ears to come to me. Be with me. But you refused to listen. You refused to see all that I had done for you. You hardened your heart and became deaf and blind to me. I was always there. If you would have only called out for me, I would have made it so that you could have seen me. Oh, the relationship that I desired with you."

"God, where am I?"

"You are on the judgment seat."

"Why am I here?'

"To be judged, of course."

"What am I being judged for?"

"The resting place for your soul's eternity lies in the balance of today's judgment, and I am afraid that I never knew you. As a result, you will be forever apart from me suffering in Hell."

"Please let me go back! Please give me another chance! I promise that I will do better."

"I am sorry Mike, but there aren't any second chances once you are on the judgment seat."

Sadly, Mike learned this bitter truth too late.

* * * *

In our society, the concept of death is not one that we enjoy discussing, and there are many good reasons why we feel this way. Death isn't pleasant. Sometimes, it can be painful or prolonged. It can ravage a person and in many cases their family as well. Funerals are usually blanketed in a cloud of sadness and for the most part only serve as a reminder that we are not immortal. When brought face to face with death, we feel afraid. Thus, we suppress the subject entirely and never consider it in any depth. But the reality is that we are all dying from the moment we are born. It is as inevitable as the setting of the sun at the end of a day. Therefore, it would make sense that you spend some time contemplating your future.

This life is just the beginning of your existence in God's creation, and despite its relatively short length, it is the most crucial part. What is done during your lifetime while on earth will directly affect where and how you spend the rest of eternity. Those who have received the free gift of salvation through Jesus Christ will be with him in heaven. Unfortunately, those who don't know Jesus Christ as their personal Lord and Savior will have to spend the remainder of their existence in complete and utter separation from him. At this point, I have a few thought-provoking questions that I would like to ask.

For those who consider themselves saved, if you died today and had to give an account of your actions to God would you be satisfied with how you are doing? Are you doing all that you could be doing to foster a relationship with him and to make him better known to those around you? For those who would not consider themselves saved, if you knew that you might die today, would you be content with the fact that you did nothing to prepare for the next step of your existence? If you aren't satisfied with leaving the end result of your final destination to fate, then I encourage you to read below. Salvation is within your grasp.

The first step is to **admit** that you are a sinner. We are all sinners. *"All have sinned and fall short of the glory of God"* (Romans 3:23 ESV). Because of our sin, we have been separated from God.

The second step is to **believe** that Jesus Christ is the son of God and that he died for your sins. He took your place on that cross. We deserve death because *"The wages of sin is death"* (Romans 6:23 ESV). But Jesus died in our place. *"God demonstrates His own love toward us, in that while we were yet sinners, Christ died for us"* (Romans 5:8 NASB). But he defeated death and rose from the dead. *"Christ died for our sins according to the Scriptures, and that He was buried, and that He rose again the third day according to the Scriptures"* (1 Corinthians 15:3-4 NKJV). He is the only way to a true relationship with God. *"Jesus said to him, 'I am the way, and the truth, and the life; no one comes to the Father but through me"* (John 14:6 NASB). He is waiting on you to open the door to your heart. *"Behold, I stand at the door and knock; if anyone hears my voice and opens the door, I will come in to him"* (Revelation 3:20 NASB).

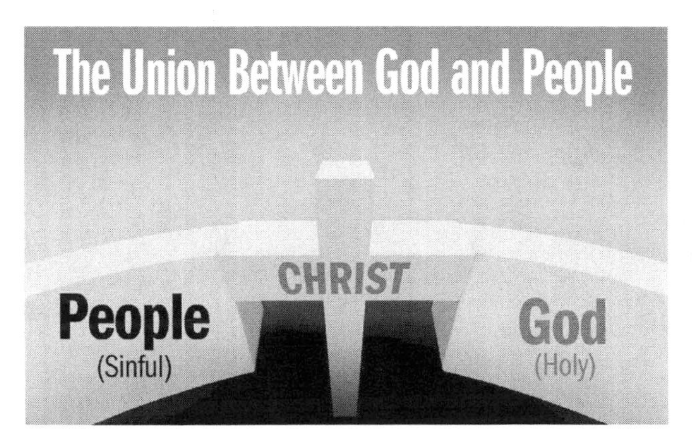

The third step is to **confess** your sins to the Lord. *"But if we confess our sins, He will forgive our sins because we can trust God to do what is right. He will cleanse us from all wrongs we have done"* (1 John 1:9 NCV).

At this point, I invite you to do this if you have not done so before. Here is a simple prayer that you can use:

"God, I am a sinner.

"Jesus, I believe that you are God's son and that you died for my sins.

"Please come into my heart and be the Lord of my life.

"And please forgive me for my sins, and help me to turn away from them."

Congratulations! If you said this prayer earnestly, you have made the biggest decision of your life. God has just washed away your sins. Acts 3:19 says, *"Repent, then, and turn to God, so that your sins may be wiped out, that times of refreshing may come from the Lord"* (NIV). Your soul is now like a newborn baby. It has been born again and is now breathing, moving, and living for the first time.

The last step is to **commit** to change. This commitment is for a lifetime, and it will require a great deal of work. Thus, I encourage you to find a church home to aid you in this process. If you need help finding one, please contact the New Hope Church of Happyville at 777-HOPE.

TWELVE

For several minutes, the examining room was quiet while Brad and his mother focused their attention on the pamphlets in their hands. During this time, the only sound to be heard was the noise that a page makes as it is being turned. After they finished, they closed their pamphlets and held them tightly against their chests. Neither acknowledged the other. They sat in silence, staring across the room while their minds processed the information they had just received.

On occasion, Brad had pondered the question of whether there was a God. Typically, this question came up when he was alone in nature. Given his circumstances at home, he spent a great deal of time outside. While there, he would contemplate various issues, and one of these issues happened to be the issue of nature itself. He had developed an appreciation for its complexity. From the soil beneath his feet to the sky overhead, he realized that nature was truly a work of great design. He saw that every creature had been made for a purpose, and if one part failed in serving its purpose, then the rest of creation suffered. Nothing had been created randomly. Rather, all of creation had been ordered down to the finest detail.

For example, he learned in school that the earth moved around the sun with exact precision. If its course was altered ever so slightly, it would quickly become too hot or cold to support life. In addition to this, he learned that the earth revolved in such a manner that without fail there was always a day, night, and four ever-recurring seasons. During the warmer months, the sky brought rain to the nutrient-enriched soil of the earth, and together the sun, water, and nutrients helped the plants grow. With the food and air that the plants provided, the moving creatures of the earth were able to survive and function properly. On a smaller scale, the plants and animals were also extremely complex. Some organisms were composed of over a trillion cells, and like nature, these cells had to work together so that the entire bodies functioned properly. It was through observations such as these that he had learned to appreciate the complexity of nature.

His teachers at school taught that the universe had formed spontaneously and then evolved over time. However, he had trouble believing this theory. He felt certain that something must have created the universe. He also suspected that this something was still caring for the earth, because it should have spun out of control long ago if man were its only caretaker. Thus, he reasoned that there had to be a God, but at the same time, he also realized that he knew very little about him. From his powers of observation, he had ascertained that God had made his creation with an unparalleled order, and within this order, every creation had been made with a purpose. From the minerals in the ground to the birds in the sky, each creation functioned to serve a higher purpose. The minerals served the plants. The plants served the animals, and atop the pyramidal scheme was mankind. The minerals, plants, and animals had been created to serve the human race.

In Brad's mind, the minerals, plants, and animals had been given a clear purpose for their existence. This realization brought him to a crossroads of sorts. A question had formed in his mind that he hadn't been able to answer. If every creation served a higher purpose, then what was man's purpose for living? If the minerals, plants, and animals had been created to serve man, then what had man been created to serve? He sensed that he had a higher purpose, but as of yet he didn't know the substance of it. His instincts told him that there had to be more to this life than what he had been currently experiencing. Otherwise, he wouldn't have pondered questions like, "Why was I created?" and "What is the purpose for living?" Thus far, his life experiences had not answered these questions but only served to expose the emptiness he felt inside.

He knew that his soul was longing for something, but he had no idea that this something was the very being who had created the world. For the most part, he had never considered why he enjoyed his walks in nature. He just knew that while in nature he felt better. What he couldn't perceive was that while in nature he had unknowingly been drawing closer to God. During his walks, his mind often drifted to heavenly matters, and when this occurred, he had entered into a time of communion with the God who had created him. It was during these moments that he had been fulfilling the purpose for which he had been made. His sole purpose, the reason why he had been created, was to have a personal relationship with his creator, and whenever he performed this purpose, whether he knew it or not, he naturally felt a sense of fulfillment. This was because the same God who had given the birds of the air the instinct to fly south for the winter and the salmon of the ocean the instinct to swim thousands of miles upstream had given man the instinct to form a relationship with his creator God.

"The Forgotten Easter" story brought Brad's experiences over the last year into a new light. Not long ago, he had questioned his purpose for living. If the "The Forgotten Easter" story was indeed true, he realized that he had just found the answer. His discovery had blessed him with a wonderful new perspective, and from it, he could see that his life was a small but important part of a larger world. Over the last year, he had begun to wonder if he was all alone, but now he realized that this wasn't true at all. He hadn't been left alone to write the chapters of his life's story. Rather, his story was essentially a part of a bigger story, and the truth was that he wasn't the author of either. The author of these stories was God, and the best part of it all was that God loved him and wanted a relationship with him.

* * * *

On the other side of the room, Mrs. Buerger sat and contemplated the story that she had just read. For Mrs. Buerger, the "CrossRoads" story had rekindled memories from her childhood. In particular, she was reminded of her family's weekly ritual of attending church. Each Sunday, her family would get out of bed and dress in their finest clothes before heading off to church. To her chagrin, this occurred every week without fail. Her father believed that his love was best displayed through acts of discipline, so he established many household rules that had consequences if broken. One of these rules was the weekly attendance of church. As with all of her father's rules, compliance wasn't optional. Because of his heavy-handedness, she had developed a rebellious streak that manifested itself through a fierce opposition to anything that he forced upon her. When she turned eighteen, she left home and never looked back. Once on her own, she rejected all of the disciplines that he had mandated, and one of those disciplines was the weekly attendance of church.

In addition to the aforementioned reason, there were other reasons why she hadn't cared for church. From her standpoint, the people who attended church were hypocrites because they never embraced the teachings that were taught. At the beginning of each sermon, the pastor would utter the statement, "He who has ears to hear, let him hear," but despite his plea, it appeared to her that no one listened. If fact, some of the men in the congregation had already drifted off to sleep by this point. Many times, their pastor had urged them to love one another, but she had never felt the warmth of love at church. Ironically, she had come to associate church with being cold and empty and not a place filled with love.

The pastor often spoke to the church about the need to give generously of their time and money. During these sermons, he would tell the congregation that where their time and money went was where their heart would be as well. He would remind them that they had been commanded to care for the poor and needy. At the conclusion of those sermons, he would always challenge the congregation to personally assess their own lives to see if their hearts were in the right place. From her seat among the pews, she surmised that no one ever responded. Otherwise, he would not have spoken on this topic with such frequency.

When not engaged on this topic, he would spend time expounding on other commandments written in the Bible. For example, he taught them that they were not to judge one another, but from her perspective, it appeared that this was the only thing that they did truly well. They seemed to never miss an opportunity to look down their noses at someone else. If that wasn't bad enough, they also loved to gossip about others' wrongdoings behind their backs. Ironically, these same people would quickly turn around and commit the very act that they had just condemned or acts that were far worse. If caught, they weren't afraid to tell a lie or slander someone if it might make them look better in the end.

But the main reason why she had stopped attending church was because she had failed to see its relevance. Aside from calling its members to live a better life, she had not seen a higher purpose. During her years of attendance, she had sensed that there had to be more than just living better. If this was its only purpose, then the church had failed miserably, and she wondered why anyone would ever keep going. Many times, she had looked for this higher purpose but had never found it. She saw others fully embrace church, but she had never felt this same connection. These individuals talked about God as if they had a close personal relationship with him.

As far as God was concerned, she did have the basic belief that there was a God, but beyond this belief, she had not delved deeper into the issue. She had never considered that God was still present, actively working in her life, and she had certainly not considered that God actually wanted to have a relationship with her.

* * * *

While both were lost in their thoughts, their family physician, Dr. Sprayberry, entered the room. Prior to reading "The Forgotten Easter" story, Brad had been very apprehensive about his arrival, but strangely enough, he realized that those worries had vanished, and in their place, a peaceful, easy feeling had settled. Brad knew that Dr. Sprayberry had the power to make him do things that he would rather not, but as a whole, he was no longer worried or concerned. In fact, he had become altogether indifferent about the prospect of being poked by another needle.

To his surprise, the visit was quite unremarkable. After hearing Mrs. Buerger's concerns about her son, Dr. Sprayberry asked a few questions of his own and then performed an examination. After completing his assessment, he concluded that Brad was suffering from exhaustion and simply needed to rest and nothing more. Brad was elated to hear this news. There would be no blood work, tests, shots or medicines. At the conclusion of the visit, Brad did something very out of character. He hopped down from the examining table and gave Dr. Sprayberry a big, heartfelt hug. His motivation wasn't because of the good news that he had just received or because Dr. Sprayberry had successfully saved his life not just once but twice. Rather, it was because of the other good news that he had just received from "The Forgotten Easter" story. If not for Dr. Sprayberry's willingness to share this news through the booklet, he might have never heard it. But Brad had not only heard the news, he had received it. And this was good news indeed, for on this day, Dr. Sprayberry had done more than help save Brad's life. He had helped save his soul.

After paying the bill, they returned to their car and headed home. Along the way, they came upon an accident in the road. Someone had been driving too fast and carelessly run through a traffic light. A collision had ensued, and sadly, it had been fatal. As a result, the traffic had been rerouted another way. Following the line of cars, Mrs. Buerger drove their car in this new direction.

They quickly came to a landmark that neither she nor Brad had ever seen. This new landmark happened to be the place where "The Forgotten Easter" and "CrossRoads" pamphlets had originated. It was the New Hope Church of Happyville. From the road, there wasn't much to see. The building was quite small, and perched atop its roof was a short steeple. The exterior of the building had been painted white, but even from the road, Brad could tell that it desperately needed a new coat of paint—the existing paint was cracked and peeling. At the entrance of the church, there were a few sparse-looking shrubs, and in the front lawn, there was a sign that read, "God loves you! Will you love him back?"

After passing by the church, Brad turned to his mother and asked her this question. "Momma, why don't we ever go to church?"

Since reading the "CrossRoads" story, his mother had been silently struggling through a few issues. The story had been working on her, tugging at her heartstrings. After witnessing the accident, the tug only became stronger. The "CrossRoads" story had affected her in a rather profound manner. It had rekindled memories of her past. Many of those memories were difficult to relive, but there were also many good memories that she had long ago forgotten.

While pondering her past, she had a couple of revelations. For starters, her estrangement from her parents had lasted for far too long. It had been her choice to leave home, yet she had always blamed her father, stating that it was his discipline that had pushed her away. Actually it had been her pride that had made her leave and kept her from returning home. She had wanted to put the sole blame on her father when she was actually the one at fault. As a child, she couldn't see that her father's rules were only meant to protect her, but now that she was a parent with a child of her own, she saw that those rules had been created for her benefit. Her father's attempts at discipline were done to keep her safe. He had only disciplined her because he wanted the best for her. As a child, she could not see the big picture behind her father's ways because her pride had blinded her.

While coming to grips with this, a shadow of sadness fell over her heart. She had let the last twenty years slip through her fingers. Those times were lost forever. The gravity of this thought overwhelmed her, and tears began streaming down her face. But amidst this sadness, she found herself holding onto the hope that her relationship with her father didn't have to remain as it was. It could indeed change. She had to believe that the decaying remains of their former relationship could be raised from the dead. She didn't know if he would take her back after all of this time, but if she never tried, she would never find out.

Overall, the "CrossRoads" story had left her with a mixture of conflicting feelings including sadness, remorse, and hope. Prior to reading the story, she had thought very little about her father, and she had definitely not considered the need for reconciliation. But, the story had rekindled old memories, and from them a desire for reconciliation had been born. She didn't know if he would feel the same way about her, but all that she could do was hope that he would. The hope for reconciliation with her earthly father wasn't all that the "CrossRoads" story had achieved. It had also instilled within her a desire to be reconciled with her heavenly father. She had been reminded of her church-going days, and as she reflected over those times, she was struck with this thought. Like with her father, she realized that she had never been in a real relationship with God. She had been present all of those years, but during that time, she had never really engaged him. She had truly never sought him out. This realization caused another great sadness to form in her heart, but like the other sadness, a glimmer of hope was born from it. From the story, she had learned that her heavenly father not only loved her but also wanted a relationship with her. At this point, she knew that it was time for her to go back and start over. It was finally time for a new beginning.

She had been struggling through these issues when Brad had asked her about going to church. When she tried to reply, no words would come. There were only tears.

When Brad saw that he had made his mother cry, he quickly asked, "Momma, did I say something wrong?"

She wiped the tears away from her face and then spoke in a voice that cracked. "No, son…you didn't say anything wrong."

After a few more minutes passed, Brad turned again and asked, "Can we go to church sometime?"

With tears still welling up in her eyes, she nodded her head and responded with a half-audible "Yes."

* * * *

Several days later, they got up and dressed for church. Because of her previous experiences with church, Mrs. Buerger was a little apprehensive about going. Even though she had no dealings with the people who attended the New Hope Church of Happyville, she still expected to be judged and condemned by them. But when they arrived, she was pleasantly surprised by what she found. From the moment that she left her car, she was warmly welcomed. As a whole, she discovered that the church was composed of men and women who were just like herself. They too were imperfect beings, struggling to find purpose and significance in an imperfect world. Amidst their struggles, they had discovered the one thing truly worthy of their efforts, and they readily shared it with her. And so it was on a cool, spring Sunday morning at the New Hope Church of Happyville that Mrs. Buerger finally found the one thing that her soul had always longed for. She found God.

THIRTEEN

For the next several nights, Brad slept like a baby. The nightmares had stopped coming, and for this break, he was exceedingly glad. He hoped that it would remain this way. Unfortunately, his respite from the nightmares was only short-lived. At 2:23 the following morning, he awoke in a cold sweat. The man in black had returned with a vengeance. His latest nightmare had been worse than anything previous. It differed from the recurrent nightmares that he had experienced. In those nightmares, he had been the target of the man in black's attacks, but in this new nightmare, he felt like an outsider watching a scene unfold. In the scene, the man in black was on a rampage, but Brad was not his target. In fact, he wasn't in the nightmare at all. Rather, the man in black was attacking a poor creature that lived under a bridge, and although Brad had never seen Denese, he knew that she was the creature in his dream. He could see that she was helpless against the man in black's attacks. As the nightmare progressed, the water in the river began to rise, and eventually, it came to a point where she could no longer hold onto the bridge's foundation. When this occurred, a torrent of water quickly washed her downstream. In the final moments before letting go, she turned back and looked deeply into his eyes. The look on her face pierced Brad's heart, for in it, he saw a plea for help that had gone unanswered. Through the whole ordeal, he had sat idly by and watched the man in black destroy her.

The remainder of the night, Brad tossed and turned in his bed. He couldn't stop thinking about Denese. He felt compelled to help her but didn't know how because he had been having his own problems with the man in black. On three separate occasions, he had tried to reach her, but despite his best efforts, each attempt had failed. In the wake of those failures, he still hadn't found a way around him. During the day, he would mope around the house as he tried to forget his new nightmare. At night, his anxiety about going to sleep would set in again. He would try to stay awake, but at some point, he would drift off into a slumber. Then he would wake up at the exact same time with the exact same nightmare. At 2:23 A.M., he would awake with Denese's image burned into his mind. The look on her face haunted him. It was a hollow expression, the type that one gets when all hope is lost. Whenever he closed his eyes, he would see this expression. It didn't matter how he tried to distract himself. He couldn't find a way to escape her gaze. Those blue eyes were always staring at him, penetrating into his heart and soul.

* * * *

Brad had lost track of time, and before long, Sunday had come again. After dressing for church, he headed for the New Hope Church of Happyville with his mother. On this particular morning, he felt very tired. The lack of sleep had begun to take its toll. He feared that he might fall asleep during the sermon. However, when the preacher stepped to the pulpit, he felt a surge of energy course through his body that helped him stay awake and focus on the preacher's words.

As this was only his second time in a church service, he knew that he still had a lot to learn. For now, he was simply trying to acclimate himself to their ways. So when the preacher began speaking about issues that were currently happening in his own life, he began nervously looking around the sanctuary. He felt quite sure that they had singled him out. He expected to find everyone staring at him, but to his surprise, no one was paying him any attention at all. They were all looking at the preacher as if he was speaking directly to them.

The sermon was about a nefarious creature named Satan whose heart had turned blacker than blackest black. At one time, this creature had been the greatest and most powerful angel ever created, but he turned on his creator, leading a rebellion in heaven. Ultimately, he was defeated by God and cast from heaven onto earth. To this day, he continues to fight against God and his creation. In this story, Brad saw some parallels with his own life. For starters, he had begun to wonder if the man in black was one of Satan's henchmen or, even worse, that he might actually be Satan himself. As he thought about this possibility, goose bumps covered his skin, and a knot formed in the pit of his stomach.

From his encounters with the man in black, Brad knew that he was out-matched, but if the man in black was indeed a demonic spirit, Brad realized that the mismatch was far worse than anything that he could have comprehended. It was a mismatch of colossal proportions. He began to relegate himself to the fact that he wanted to help Denese but couldn't. The odds against him were simply too great. There was no way that he could expect to battle against Satan and win. Only God had the power to defeat him. By this point in the sermon, his attention had drifted away from the pastor because he had allowed his mind to become consumed by these thoughts. It wasn't until he heard a chorus of "Amens" from the congregation that he redirected his focus back to the preacher. The preacher had begun to speak on a slightly different topic. He was still talking about Satan, but he no longer talked about his power. Rather, he was speaking about God and how Satan was powerless against him. He spoke in such a way as to imply that the war with Satan had already been fought and won by God. Then he said something that filled his soul with a great deal of hope. From the pulpit, the preacher proclaimed, "If God is for us, no one can stand against us! This means that not even Satan himself can stand against us if God is at our side!"

As he contemplated the ramifications of such a statement, the fear that had overcome him began quickly dissipating. In its place, a myriad of new thoughts regarding the man in black began to spring forth. By all accounts, they were crazy and reckless. He tried to dismiss them, but they kept returning to the forefront of his mind. On the way home, he kept pondering them, and by the time his mother pulled their car into the driveway, he knew what he had to do. After changing out of his church clothes, Brad kissed his mother on the cheek and then grabbed his raincoat. As he left, his mother asked where he was going. In response, he turned, smiled, and said, "To help a friend," and then quickly walked away.

Brad gathered his bike and headed out as he had done many times before. At the halfway point, he passed the place where the crows usually roosted. He wasn't surprised when he saw that they had not left their perch. His arrival created quite a flurry of activity. They began to excitedly call to one another. Many of them started moving about, jumping from one branch to the next. On his previous trips, the crows had remained in the trees when he had passed, but today, they took flight and followed him on his journey. He tried his best to ignore them by keeping his eyes focused straight ahead. On this day, his battle wasn't with them.

As he moved closer, he developed some apprehension about his encounter with the man in black. He was about to pick a fight with a far superior foe. Even worse, he didn't have a plan of attack. He knew that this could end very poorly, but despite this potential outcome, he had already decided that he was willing to risk it all. This showdown was about more than just helping Denese. He also needed to do this for himself. He couldn't keep living in a state of perpetual fear. The time had come for him to face his fears head on. He hoped that in the process the man in black's hold over him would be broken. He realized that he couldn't do this alone, and so he was counting on God to show up and help him. As he neared the bridge, he kept repeating this phrase to himself: "If God is for me, who can stand against me? If God is for me, who can stand against me?"

By now, he was almost there. Only one hill stood between him and the man in black. Tightening his grip on the handlebars, he began peddling faster. When he crested the hill, he saw the man in black standing far ahead. He was in the middle of the road waiting for him. Brad didn't slow down this time. In fact, he peddled faster, picking up more and more speed as he went. When he was about fifty yards away from the man in black, Brad started screaming at the top of his lungs.

He didn't know what to expect, but what happened next was greater than anything that he could have imagined. From above, a beautiful, radiant ray of sunlight broke through the clouds. For a split-second, he took his eyes off of the man in black and looked towards the sky. The clouds and flock of crows had parted, and through them, a single ray of light was majestically descending upon him. Through the hole in the clouds, he saw a glimpse of blue sky. Then he saw something fall from the sky. At first, the object was a pinpoint in the skyline, but as it quickly approached his position, it began to grow rapidly in size. As it drew closer, he realized that it was an eagle. In fact, it was the largest eagle that he had ever seen. As it neared the flock of crows, it emitted an ear-piercing scream and flew directly into the black mass, causing the birds to disperse in all directions. From there, the eagle descended toward him, maintaining a position only a few feet above his head. For a moment, it slowed its pace as it examined Brad with one of its glassy eyes. Then it let off a second ear-piercing scream and began flapping its wings again, picking up speed and passing ahead of him on a course for the man in black. The space between the eagle and the man in black closed rapidly. In amazement, Brad watched as the eagle flew directly into the man in black. But there was no collision. The man in black simply vanished into a puff of black smoke and was no more. Only the eagle remained after their encounter. Brad was still coasting on his bike when this occurred. A few moments later, he passed through the area where the man in black had been standing. To his amazement, he had passed through untouched. He had come to battle the man in black, but in the end, he hadn't lifted even a finger. All that he had done was call upon the name of the Lord, and then God had come and fought for him. Brad slowed his bike to a stop. Then he sat and watched as the eagle flew away. With long, graceful flaps of its wings, the eagle slowly returned to its rightful place in the sky. It continued on its ascent until it had reached the very place where the sun had broken through the clouds, and then it passed to the other side and disappeared. Then the hole in clouds began to grow smaller and smaller until all of the blue sky disappeared as well.

From the sky, Brad looked down the muddy road leading to the bridge. As of yet, he had still not reached his final destination, so he began peddling his bike again. At the top of the hill, he stopped momentarily to look over the valley. In the center of his vision, he saw the old, broken bridge, and for the record, he had never been so happy to see it still standing. Mounting his bike again, he quickly zoomed down the hill, completing the final leg of his journey.

At the bridge, Brad jumped off his bike and ran to the hole in its floor. He began shouting, "Denese…Denese…Are you down there?"

To his relief, he heard her voice billowing up from underneath the bridge. "Yes, Brad…I'm still here. But I have a question for you: Where have you been, my old friend? I have missed you."

Then beginning with his first encounter with the man in

black, Brad told Denese about everything that had occurred over the last several weeks. As he recounted every detail, Denese listened patiently. When he finally finished, Denese broke her silence by saying, "Brad that is quite a tale. Now, please tell me what you have really been doing?"

Surprised by Denese's response, Brad responding by saying, "Denese, I'm telling you the truth. Don't you believe me?"

"No, I don't."

A long, uncomfortable pause followed Denese's blunt response. After a time of silence, Brad asked, "Which part?"

"Well, I guess that I don't believe any of it. I'm just amazed that you thought that I would. Brad, I may live under a bridge, but I'm not a fool. I know when someone is trying to con me. Besides I have been here this whole time, and I haven't seen another living soul except you. This means that I haven't seen a man who wears black and is apparently out to get me. And that bit about God sounds real nice. In fact, it sounds too nice, and anything that sounds too good to be true usually ends up not being true at all. Brad, you have a good heart, but you are too gullible. If you don't watch out, people will take advantage of you."

Brad was demoralized by Denese's remarks. For several weeks, he had been trying to reach her, but because of the man in black, he had been unable to do so. Now, after many trials and tribulations, he had finally made it back to the bridge. Needless to say, this welcome was not what he had expected. For some reason, he had led himself to believe that Denese would receive his message with open arms. When she didn't, he was overcome with feelings of disappointment, but even worse, her doubts had made him question his own beliefs. He hated to admit it but none of this made any sense. He realized that his story was quite preposterous. Yet he couldn't deny how much better he felt since God had filled the void in his life, and then there was the miracle that he had just witnessed on the road to the bridge. After taking these thoughts into consideration, the doubts that had begun to swirl in his mind began quieting down.

Then an intriguing thought popped into his head. It was so unique that he suspected that it had to be from God. It was an idea with the potential to help both of them. It would require some courage on his part to be tested. But in the process, he hoped that his faith would be strengthened and that Denese's doubts would be eradicated.

Turning to the hole in the bridge, Brad posed this question to Denese. "Denese, are you a troll?"

There was a short pause followed by a barely audible "Yes."

"Denese, how do you know that you are a troll?"

"What do you mean? I'm just a troll. This is the way that I was born. Just like a puppy is born a dog, I was born a troll."

"I mean who told you that you were a troll? Was it your father or someone else?"

After thinking about this for a moment, Denese replied, "To be honest, I don't really remember. Why are you asking?"

"Denese, I want to see you. In fact, I need to see what you look like with my own eyes."

"Brad, please don't ask me to do that. You know how I feel about this."

"I know, but this is something that I have to do. If you don't come up here, then I'm coming down there. It's your choice, but one way or another I'm going to take a look at you."

"But..."

"No buts...I'm not taking a 'No' for an answer."

"FINE...but I'm warning you that you will be sorry. Well, I'm not going to make this easy for you. If you want to see me, then you're going to have to come down here. "

"OK, if that's what you want."

Brad ran back to the roadbed and began searching for a way underneath the bridge. Rather quickly, he discovered a small, narrow, overgrown path that led the way. Once underneath the bridge, he began surveying the area, and what he saw only made his heart break. He was saddened that any creature had to live in these conditions. As he moved forward, he found Denese sitting on the ground just ahead of him with her head hidden between her knees. She didn't appear very ominous. As he had never met a troll, he didn't know what to expect. For some reason, he had created a mental image of a creature that was much larger than the one sitting in front of him. Despite her lack of size, Brad decided that it was probably best if he approached with caution. As he moved closer, Brad heard a familiar sound. It was the same sound he had heard on his first trip to the bridge. It was the sound of crying, and this sound made his heart break all the more because he knew that it was coming from Denese. After pausing momentarily to listen, Brad inched ever closer. As he approached, Denese remained sitting with her head hanging low. He knelt next to her. Then he extended his arm gently touching her shoulder with his hand. Up to this point, Denese's body had appeared altogether lifeless, but her posture changed once touched. Upon feeling the warmth of Brad's hand, Denese finally lifted up her head to greet him, and when she did, she found a heartfelt smile waiting on her.

For a moment, no words were spoken. There was just silence as they peered into each other's eyes. In Brad's eyes, Denese saw something she had long been without. She saw the qualities of love, mercy, compassion, and kindness. In Denese's eyes, Brad saw something quite different. In her eyes, Brad saw the same look he had seen in his dream. Those eyes held a look of extreme pain, confusion, and hopelessness. As they looked at one another, Brad felt the sudden urge to give Denese a hug, so he leaned forward and placed his arms around her neck. Then he gave her a big, long squeeze. At first, Denese didn't reciprocate, but in due time, she unfolded her arms and placed them around Brad's torso. Then for a brief moment in time, they continued to hold their embrace. From the surface, this embrace may have appeared as only a simple hug, but the truth is that this embrace was far more than just a hug. For both, this embrace was proof that a miracle was in the process of being made.

Looking at Denese, Brad proclaimed, "Don't you see that you and I are the same? We are no different. If you are a troll, then we are all trolls, but the truth is that you're not a troll at all. You are one-hundred percent human."

"That is a lie! There is no way that I am human. I'm a troll. I've always been one, and there is nothing that you could say that would convince me otherwise."

In that moment, another thought popped into Brad's mind. Grabbing Denese by the arm, he started tugging and pulling on her. "What are you doing?" Denese asked.

"You'll see. Just follow me." Then Brad led Denese down to the river's edge. Pointing at the water, he said, "Look!" Denese peered into the rippled, muddy water and saw the faint reflection of two faces. Brad's refection was on the left while hers glimmered in the water just next to it. As she studied her image, she began touching her face to see if the image was indeed real and not a figment of her imagination.

From the water, Denese turned to Brad and looked deep into his eyes. Then with a look of disbelief on her face, she asked, "How can that be? A creature can't simply change who it is. A troll can't just become human."

"Denese, I don't believe that you were ever a troll. You have been told so many lies that you started believing that they were true. As far as change goes, I once believed as you, but I now realize that change can occur. I have seen it in my own life and in the lives of my family. Even if you were a troll, I believe that you still have the ability to change."

Shaking her head, Denese responded by saying, "I don't

know. This is really too much. I don't know if I can believe it, much less bear it. To have believed that I was a troll for all of these years when, in fact, I was not is almost more than my heart can take. Think of all the time that was wasted. Think of all of the needless pain that I felt." Denese kept shaking her head while muttering, "I don't know. I just don't know." Then she looked up at Brad and said, "I wish that you had never brought this to my attention. I would like to forget the whole thing and go back to the way things were. I believe that I would rather think that I was a troll than have to face the prospect of changing. This is the only life that I know. I'm comfortable here. I believe that change would just be too hard for me."

"Denese, how can you say that? Do you really want to continue living in this manner? Is living under a bridge all that you hope to achieve in this life? Can't you see that there is a better way?"

"Quite honestly, I can't. Brad, I believe that you mean well, but I would like for you to leave. And I want you to say goodbye to this place because I don't want to see you again."

From the tone in her voice, Brad knew that she was serious. He started to plead with Denese over this matter, but she stopped him before he could begin. Then she quietly pointed towards the path signifying that she was ready for him to leave. Before leaving, he tried to give her one last heartfelt look, but she had already walked away. Brokenhearted, he slowly made his way back up the path. At the foot of the bridge, he took a moment to say goodbye. Then he mounted his bike and headed home.

As Brad peddled home, he reflected over the events that had just transpired. In his whole life, he had never experienced such a wide range of emotions. When he approached the man in black, he felt deathly afraid, but after the eagle had descended from the sky and granted him victory, he was filled with an immeasurable sense of joy. Next, his heart had been filled with love after sharing an embrace with Denese. However, these feelings had been washed away, and in their place, only a sense of rejection remained. He had never cared for someone as he had Denese. In fact, he was shocked as to how deeply he cared for her. His love for her had driven him to fight for her in ways that he didn't know were possible. As he peddled home from the bridge, he realized that all of his efforts had been for naught, and in the end, he hadn't really accomplished anything.

* * * *

The following morning, he awoke to the sound of thunder echoing in the distance. When the sound grew louder, he got out of bed to investigate the commotion in the sky. High above, ominous looking rain clouds were moving in his direction. While he watched, several flashes of lightning streaked across the horizon. Fascinated by the size and power of the approaching storm, he decided to take a seat and watch the scene unfold. Several minutes later, the leading edge of the storm reached their house. As it approached, the light from the sky grew dim. This was followed by a series of wind gusts that shook the foundation of their house and the trees that surrounded it. Following the wind gusts, large raindrops began to fall in thick sheets from the sky. Very quickly, the sky and surrounding countryside were blotted out, and in their place, only the gray-white of rain remained.

The storm continued throughout the day and into the night. The following day, the storm kept pouring out its wrath onto the earth below. For three straight days, the storm continued its attack on the countryside of Happy Land and, in particular, the town of Happyville. Prior to this storm, Happy Land had already been thoroughly soaked. The ground was soggy and squishy, and the rivers were flowing at maximum capacity. The land could not receive the heavy deluge of rain that was falling from the sky. With nowhere to go, the water started to accumulate on the ground. At first, it began to form large puddles, but over time, the puddles began to coalesce into larger pools. As time progressed, rivers began to form in places where rivers should not have formed. In the end, the whole town of Happyville found that it was under siege by a great flood, the likes of which they had never known. Homes and stores were flooded. Even the local churches discovered that they had not been spared from the wrath of the flood's damaging waters.

During this time, Brad thought of Denese often. Even though Denese had rejected him, he still cared for her well-being. He feared for her safety given the degree of flooding that had occurred. On several occasions, he found himself reflecting over his last nightmare and wondering if Denese had actually been swept away by the river's rising waters. In the pit of his stomach, he developed a sinking suspicion that she had indeed been carried away. She had told him not to come back to the bridge, but he couldn't sit idly and do nothing. The suspense was driving him crazy, and he knew that this feeling wouldn't go away until he checked on her. So he decided to visit the bridge again. After retrieving his raincoat, he got his bike and headed for the bridge one last time.

The going was very slow because large amounts of free-standing water had accumulated on the roadbed. When he finally arrived, he found that the river was overflowing its banks. Walking gingerly on the bridge, Brad moved to the hole where he had often conversed with Denese. Typically, the river was a good distance below the hole, but as he peered into it, he discovered that the river was just a few feet away. He quickly realized that there was no way that Denese could still be under the bridge. From there, he moved back to the road and started calling out her name. When there was no response, he moved to either side of the bridge and began calling out for her again. When there was still no response, his concern for her only intensified. A foreboding feeling began to fill his heart, and in that instant, he knew that something terrible had happened. Instinctively, he began running downstream. He hoped to find her intact and doing well, but deep down, he feared that this would not be the case. As he ran, he tried to prepare himself for the worst.

He maneuvered his way down the riverbank as quickly as he could. At times when passing through grassy sections, the walking was easy, but then at other times, he would find the walking to be difficult and tedious as he passed through sections that were filled with shrubs and briar patches. As he went, the number and length of the grassy sections began to diminish greatly. Then at some point, the grassy sections ceased coming altogether, leaving only briars, thorns, and thistles in his path. Despite these obstacles, he continued onward with the hopes of finding her. But as the distance from the bridge grew in length, his hope of finding her alive began shrinking. At every turn of the river, he had started holding his breath in anticipation of what he might find. He feared that he would round one of the bends in the river and find Denese's body washed ashore.

Much to his displeasure, this discovery was indeed what happened. After passing a large bend in the river, he saw a small figure in the water. Immediately, he knew that the figure in the water had to be Denese. Quickening his pace, he moved to her location. He found her lying face down in the water, and even though he couldn't see her face, he knew that it was her body. She had become lodged in a tree that had fallen into the river. The current briskly moved over and around her body causing her arms to sway back and forth in the water. He plunged into the icy-cold river after her. The wading was difficult because even at the river's edge the currents were powerful. At one point, he feared that he might be swept downstream. But despite all of this, he continued onward. After reaching her body, he extracted her from the tree branches and slowly dragged her onto shore. Then he turned her face up and collapsed on the riverbank next to her. Overwhelmed with grief, he fell upon her cold, lifeless body and began crying uncontrollably.

PART TWO

PART TWO

John Bunyan's *Pilgrim's Progress* has been one of the most influential books ever written. It has remained in print for over three centuries and has been published in over 100 languages. For many generations, *Pilgrim's Progress* was, after the Bible, the most deeply cherished book in the Christian home. The following excerpt is from the apology that began this classical work.

"When at the first I took my pen in hand
Thus for to write, I did not understand
That I at all should make a little book
In such a mode; nay, I had undertook
To make another; which when almost done,
Before I was aware, I this begun
And thus it was: I, writing of the way
And race of saints in this our Gospel-day,
*Fell suddenly into an **allegory***
About their journey, and the way to glory..."

John Bunyan had not intended to write an allegory, but this is what poured from his heart. In a similar fashion, I had never intended to write an allegory, but when I put pen to paper, this is what resulted.

An allegory is a work in which the characters and events are understood to be symbolic and carry a deeper meaning than portrayed. The story that began this book is an allegory. It is the telling of tale that occurred in my life several years ago. It was written and for a time put down, only to be picked up again at a later date. The story is about a homeless woman named Denese whom I met underneath a bridge, our friendship, and the trials that resulted. I began this work not knowing how it would end. I simply wrote as the Spirit led. Many of the chapters were inspired as the actual events were unfolding. You might say that it was an actual work in progress...that is until Denese died. When she died, the story ended. Needless to say, this was not what I had hoped would happen.

For several years, the story lay dormant. It was unfinished, so I didn't share it with anyone. In my heart, I sensed that there had to be more. I had trouble believing that it was simply over. But what do you do when one of the main characters dies? I could have finished the work by giving it a different ending, but then it wouldn't have held true with the storyline. Ultimately, I decided to do nothing. I put the story down and waited, not knowing if it would ever be worked on again.

Over the years, I have learned that waiting is one of the most powerful acts that a follower of Christ can do. The act of waiting is so contrary to the American mindset. Like many, I am a doer. I want to see results instantly. I believe that God likes to give doers tasks that they can't finish on our own. By doing so, he forces us to wait on him. My life verse has become Psalm 46:10 for this very reason. It helps me to remember my place in God's universe. It reads, *"Be still, and know that I am God. I will be exalted among the nations, I will be exalted in the earth!"* (ESV) Too often, I try to please God by busying myself with activities that I think will please him when, in reality, this may not be what he desires of me. There are times he simply wants me to be still and wait. He is big enough to handle the world's problems. In fact, he may not just handle them. He might chose to do something miraculous instead.

King Solomon wrote in Ecclesiastes that there is a season for all things. There is *"a time to keep silent and time to speak."* For this story, the time of waiting has ended. I have been still. God has done his part. Now it is time to speak. The remainder of this section will be dedicated to the telling of Denese's true story, my small part in it, and the miracle that ensued after her death.

* * * *

A Bridge…

I will never forget the first day that I met Denese. It was a cool, bright November afternoon. I am a physician, and I had just finished volunteering at the Good News Clinic, our local medical clinic for the indigent. At the time, my normal routine was to share a morning devotional with the patients in the waiting room and then to give them a sack lunch to take along for the day. On this particular occasion, I made one request of those in attendance. I had a service project weighing heavy on my heart, and I needed their help. Thanksgiving was quickly approaching, and I wanted to provide a meal for someone who might not get one otherwise. I asked them if they knew of a family or group that fit this description. Several in the group answered, and interestingly enough, their answers were all the same. They mentioned a group of men and women who lived underneath a nearby bridge. I realized that I knew this place. It was only a few blocks away. I had driven over it countless times but had never stopped to consider that someone might actually live there.

In general, I do not believe in coincidence, so when three separate people gave me the same answer, I considered this to be a sign. After the morning clinic was over, I decided to go on a reconnaissance mission. On the way, I stopped at Burger King to purchase a sack full of hamburgers. I had no idea what might await me there. I reasoned that it couldn't hurt to bring along some food. Once I arrived, I realized that I didn't know how to get down there. I drove over the bridge a few times before deciding to park and explore. I walked through the woods, climbed across a stream, and passed by the remains of what was once known as "Tent City." The ground was littered with debris. Torn tents and broken chairs were strewn everywhere. But there were no people. My anxiety began to mount as I walked through this forgotten wasteland. I kept moving and happened upon a middle-aged black man. He was sitting alone in the only tent left standing. I spoke to him for a minute or so. Then, in exchange for a couple of hamburgers, he kindly pointed me in the right direction. I would learn later that this gentleman suffered with schizophrenia and chose to live in solitude because he was prone to violent outbursts.

Following his directions, I continued along the path and eventually emerged from the woods. After crossing a set of railroad tracks and a dry streambed, I finally made it to the bridge. From where I stood, the bridge crossed over my head. Its steel girders ran parallel to the road. Three large concrete footings, each six feet wide, formed its foundation. Large rocks covered the hill that sloped down from the top. The rocks were covered with trash, mostly beer cans. There was a small path etched into the left side of the hill. At the top, just underneath the bridge, rudimentary living quarters had been made. Blankets and tarps created walls. Cardboard boxes substituted as beds. Garbage bags filled with clothes served as closets. At the base of the hill, a couple of old couches sat next to a fire contained within a rusty fifty-gallon drum, creating the illusion of a cozy den.

A great sadness fell over my heart upon seeing this sight. I had no idea that human beings in my hometown lived in this way. Gainesville, Georgia, after all, is a relatively small town. It isn't Atlanta, New York, or Los Angeles. You expect poverty in those larger metropolitan cities but not in Gainesville. It is a quiet, affluent town with a population of 35,000 located in the rolling foothills of north Georgia. It is a far cry from those larger cities, or so I had led myself to believe. As I took it in, I realized that Gainesville was no different; poverty existed here as well. I had not seen it because I had not been looking. I had been living in a state of blissful ignorance. I had not wanted to acknowledge the trials of my fellow man. I remember feeling guilty. I had been blessed with so much. I had a home, clothes, and food. In stark contrast, these people had none of these things.

From these thoughts, my attention was drawn back up the hill to where several people had begun moving. They seemed unaware of my presence. They were talking amongst themselves while moving in and out of their little personal spaces or "cuts" as they liked to call them. I decided that it was time to go up and meet them, so I carefully navigated my way up the rocky path. As I entered into their home, I tried to be as courteous as possible. The first person that I met was a young man named Derek. He was lounging on an old mattress. I offered him a couple of hamburgers and then sat and talked with him for a few minutes. I worked my way across the underside of the bridge, saying hello, shaking hands, and offering a hamburger to those that I met. At the far side, I came upon a woman sitting on the ground with her knees pulled up to her chest. She had red hair and blue eyes. She was smoking a cigarette. Her left arm was in a brace because of an injury sustained during a recent fall. I knelt down next to her, introduced myself, and then asked her name. She said, "My name is Denese." We talked for a short time and then said our goodbyes. In retrospect, the significance of this moment had passed by unnoticed. I did not realize that a friendship had been birthed that God would use to touch not only my life but others halfway across the world.

Denese

In the following weeks, I returned several times to visit and bring food. I also brought along my best friend and partner in ministry, Clint Anderson. For several years, we had been working together doing a ministry called the ARK Project. ARK is an acronym that stands for Acts of Real Kindness. Every couple of weeks, we would venture out into our community to do service projects. For our next project, we had chosen to do the Thanksgiving feeding that I had mentioned previously. We were laying the groundwork by making connections and spreading the word that we would be back on Thanksgiving to bring them dinner. When the day arrived, we brought tables, chairs, and the very same meal that you or I might sit down to eat. It was a wonderful occasion. We left knowing that we had shown God's love through this simple act of kindness.

Typically, we did not return to the same venue twice to perform a service project, but something had changed inside both Clint and me. God had laid the men and women who lived under the bridge on our hearts, and we couldn't shake the feeling that he was calling us to go back. So we put the ARK Project on hold and decided to return to the bridge each week instead. We would bring a simple meal and then talk to them while we ate together. We shared our stories, and then they shared theirs. We learned that we weren't very different. We were all sinners in need of God's grace.

In fact, after hearing their stories, Clint and I realized that we could have easily ended up living under a bridge if we had been forced to walk in their shoes. Their stories were heartbreaking. Most were raised in abusive, broken homes where substance abuse and mental illness were the norm. Most had been in prison before the age of twenty, and with criminal records, it had become nearly impossible for them to find gainful employment. None had support groups they could fall back on. For some, these people had never existed. It was a sad situation. They were stuck, and they knew it. Most had turned to alcohol or drugs to numb the pain, and after years of abuse, they were now badly addicted. Mental illnesses such as bipolar disorder, schizophrenia, and depression were prevalent among the group. Some probably came by it honestly, having inherited it from their parents. Others cultivated it through their depraved lifestyle. Either way, mental illness only added to the complexity of their hopeless situation.

As Clint and I battled with how to best help these men and women, we decided to do for them what God would do for us. We would love them exactly where they were. Of course, we wanted to see them get better. We hoped that one day they would move away from the bridge to live normal lives, but we were also realistic. Many had lived there for years and had seen countless church groups and other charitable organizations come and go. Besides, we weren't equipped to rehabilitate them even if they wanted it. Our mission would have to be much simpler. We decided that this outreach would be an extension of the ARK Project. On a regular basis, we would show them the love of Jesus

Christ. This would be the starting point upon which we would build our ministry. As it would turn out, we would have to return to this basic tenet time and time again.

...A Church...

After a couple of months of outreach, Clint and I had a crazy idea. Few, if any, of the men and women attended church. We suspected that they were too ashamed to go. On the street, they fit in and thus were easily overlooked, but in church, they stuck out like a sore thumb. The fact that they felt unaccepted by the one institution that should have readily embraced them grieved our hearts. We felt God calling us to do something radical. If they wouldn't go to church, then we would just take it to them. We organized an ARK Project to clean up the bridge. One person built a large cross and cemented it in the ground. Another built an altar rail and kneeling bench. Then, each Sunday at four o'clock sharp, we arrived. We brought a meal, tables and chairs, music equipment, and a PA system. We fed their stomachs, and after they were full, we fed their souls. There was a time of praise and worship followed by a sermon given by Clint or myself. After the service, we gave them small items such as toothbrushes or deodorant to help them through their week. Of all the items that we gave out, their favorite, by far, was the weekly distribution of tickets for the local bus transit. As I was the one who always gave them away, I dubiously earned the nickname "bus pass man."

Word of our outreach, which had taken on the name The Bridge Ministry, began spreading throughout the community. People became very interested and started asking questions. They too were surprised to know that there were homeless men and women living under a bridge in their hometown. Some were shocked, left wondering what kind of person would live under a bridge. I always suspected that those individuals envisioned the people that I described as being troll-like, not actually real persons. Others warmed to our calling and took it upon themselves to aid us in it. People started coming to our weekly church service. They helped prepare meals, which was a huge blessing because neither of us could cook. But, the biggest blessing was the arrival of musicians. Neither of us had a lick of musical talent. The best that we could muster was a joyful noise. We gladly gave over this duty. Whatever we needed, God always provided. On most Sundays, it was a small crowd of ten to twenty, but on a few occasions it might swell up to fifty or sixty. Regardless of the weather, we went. Extreme heat or cold, rain or snow, threat of lightning or tornado didn't stop us. Neither did the awful smells originating from the poultry plant next door.

Our time on Sundays turned into more than just a church service. It became an outreach opportunity for the community, forming a bridge between two groups of people who otherwise would have never met. Men, women, and children would volunteer their time and talents. They participated in the church services by singing, teaching, giving testimonies, or sitting in the pews. It was a beautiful sight to see upper middle class America blending in with the poorest of the poor. On one occasion, I preached about when Jesus washed the disciples' feet. It was an act of great love and humility for the teacher to wash his pupils' feet, especially when your teacher was the Son of God. At the end, we washed each other's feet. I remember having the privilege of washing Denese's feet. She objected and blushed the entire time. This was one simple example of how we tried to show them love while also teaching them. Change came slowly for those living under the bridge. It was just the opposite for the volunteers. To my surprise, the greatest change occurred in this group. They were deeply touched by their experiences under the bridge. We even had a few regulars who never missed. Each week, they would come and pour their hearts and souls into the bridge folks.

...A Growing Relationship...

As the ministry grew, my relationship with Denese grew as well. My wife, Meredith, and our two children, Hunter and Halle, started coming to the bridge service. They instantly fell in love with Denese, especially my wife. She and Denese began forming a tight bond. Meredith would pick her up during the week and take her out to lunch. Around this time, we started bringing her to church with us on Sunday mornings. She also came to our home to do odd jobs, mostly cleaning. We had no idea how useful a simple toothbrush could be for cleaning those hard to get places until she showed us for the first time.

As our friendship grew, we earned the right to speak more openly to her about her lifestyle. We knew that she was killing herself. She had been living under the bridge for years, and the time had begun to take its toll. She was in her late forties but looked a good ten years older. At one time, she had been addicted to methamphetamines, but after spending time in prison, she was able to kick this habit. Unfortunately, she had only replaced one bad habit with another. She had turned to alcohol instead. Each day, she would drink large quantities of alcohol just to keep from withdrawing. We knew that if she was to get better this cycle had to end.

We encouraged her to enter a rehab program, but she was resistant to the idea. She had plenty of reasons, none of which were valid. The bottom line was that she wasn't ready to go. Her ties to the bridge were too strong. Her entire life had become wrapped up in its dangerous web. Under the bridge, she could feed her addiction without judgment. Besides, all of her friends and worldly possessions were there. She knew the risks of staying under the bridge, but she was more frightened of living apart from it. We continued to gently encourage her, reassuring her that there was a better life on the other side. Eventually, she gave in, at least partially. We wanted her to go to a rehab far away from the bridge. She agreed to go through detox at our local mental health clinic. Afterwards, she stayed at a boarding house less than a mile from the bridge. We were less than thrilled but still considered her decision a huge victory. She did well for a time. In fact, she remained sober for almost three months, but one night her roommate sneaked in some alcohol, and from there it went downhill quickly. By the end of the week, she was back under the bridge. Meredith was devastated, and to protect herself, she pulled away.

Meanwhile, Clint and I continued to minister to Denese and the others each Sunday afternoon. Rather than improve, the conditions only worsened. The bridge folks usually tried to sober up for the bridge service, but when Denese returned, they abandoned this habit altogether. When we arrived each week, they would already be heavily intoxicated. The group had become loud, argumentative, and at times almost combative. When Denese left, there was a sense of hope that someone might escape.

When she returned, this hope was extinguished. It seemed as if they had given up.

There were newcomers to the bridge on a weekly basis, some less savory than others. At times, I could feel the palpable presence of evil lurking in our midst. This sensation was the most intense when a man wearing a black trench coat would show up. His hatred towards me was intense even though I had done nothing to warrant it. The bridge folks told me that he had expressed a desire to kill me on several occasions. Needless to say, I had developed some anxiety about going to the bridge. This feeling would mount throughout the week, and if he did show up on Sundays, it would hit a feverish peak. Ultimately, I had to reach a point where I simply trusted in God to protect me. I had to put my fears behind me and continue the work at hand. There were a couple of occasions when I thought that he might attack, but thank God, he never laid a finger on me.

In the wake of her failed rehab, Denese started drinking even more than usual. She had become a powder keg of emotions. One minute, she would be laughing and the next crying. Then there were moments when her temper would flare uncontrollably. She would spout off a series of obscenities and in the next breath ask for forgiveness. In addition to her growing mental and emotional instability, her health began deteriorating right before my very eyes. She developed signs of pneumonia, so I sent her to the Good News Clinic for treatment. While there, one of my colleagues evaluated the condition of her liver. He performed an examination and ordered some blood work. After reviewing the results, he called me. Her liver was failing, and if she didn't stop drinking, she would be dead within a year.

Around this time, I received another phone call regarding Denese. This call came from a local pastor named Loren Hildebrant. He had heard about our ministry and decided to venture down to the bridge on his own. Like me, he met Denese and fell in love with her. He quickly developed some concerns about her health, so he took it upon himself to find her another rehab facility. Using some of his connections, he located one in south Georgia that would take her for free. The only problem was that she didn't want to go. This was the reason why Loren had called. He needed my help. We had to convince Denese to go back to rehab. The following Sunday, I talked with her about this topic. I could see the fear in her eyes. She was afraid that she would fail again, and she didn't want to let everyone, including herself and God, down again. To me, the decision was a simple one, but in her mind, it was much more complicated. The weight of our hopes for her wore heavy upon her shoulders. Her past failure had sent her crashing down. She had many regrets over letting everyone and especially her own children down. She didn't know if she could handle another disappointment, even if it meant a premature death.

Over the next several weeks, we continued working on her, and eventually, she agreed to go. Then Loren and I set a date when we would met and extract her from the bridge. We feared that she would change her mind at the last minute, but this was not the case. She came willingly. The folks under the bridge gave her a heartfelt sending off as she walked away. At the road, Meredith and I gave her a hug and wished her well. We couldn't go any further with her on this day. We had a prior engagement, one that had been planned for months, and we couldn't miss it. About nine months prior, we had volunteered for a medical mission trip. Soon we would be heading to Africa to visit a small country called Uganda. We had an appointment at the health department to get our vaccinations. This one remark sparked a rather interesting conversation. As it would turn out, Loren was leading his church on a medical mission trip to Uganda as well. Curiously, they were leaving on the exact same week as our trip. I remember walking away in disbelief. I couldn't fathom the odds of such an encounter.

At this point, I had no idea that God was up to something big.

...A Mission Trip...

For several years, God had been working on me about going on a mission trip, but I had avoided the subject, using the excuse that there was enough work to be done in my local community. Eventually, I relented of this viewpoint after reading a book entitled *Radical*. I called the last person who had asked me to go on a mission trip and finally said yes. This was in the summer of 2010. The trip was scheduled for March of the following year. Even though I was following God's calling, I still felt very anxious about my decision. This would be my first experience on the mission field. Practicing medicine in my clinic was easy. I could order any test, prescribe any medication, or refer to any consultant that the patient needed. Performing this same job in an environment where none of this existed was a different story altogether. In the time leading up to the trip, I tried to ready myself, but in the back of my mind, I developed this growing realization that no amount of preparation would prepare me for what I would encounter. As the months turned into weeks, my apprehension only grew more intense.

The day I met Loren at the bridge my mission trip was only four weeks away. Needless to say, a great deal of planning had gone into it by this point. I had taken time off from work. Plane tickets had been purchased. Vaccinations had been administered. Anti-malarial medications had been obtained. Letters for support, asking for donations for medical supplies, had been sent and received. The team had been assembled. Everything was on schedule, and then it just fell apart. The team dropped to only five members seemingly overnight. The worst part was that I was the only medical professional on the trip. Nine months ago, I had signed up for a medical mission trip. With three weeks left, I was all that remained of a promising group of doctors and nurses. My anxiety went through the roof. I envisioned myself being swallowed by a sea of patients wanting medical care. I knew that I wasn't ready to tackle something of this magnitude on my own. I didn't know what to do.

When this occurred, I turned to God. I felt like I was in this predicament because of his constant nudging. In my prayers, I reminded him of this fact. I wondered if he had forsaken me. In retrospect, I should have never doubted him. He has always been faithful to me. As it would turn out, he had already found a solution for my problem, but I would still need a little help in visualizing it. For a couple of months, my mother-in-law had wanted me to meet with a former medical missionary who attended her church. She had felt very strongly about this, so she arranged a meeting at her home. The timing was impeccable. I had just met with Loren the week prior. Shortly thereafter, I had received the bad news about the mission trip. At this point, I found myself sitting in my mother-in-law's home with a dentist who had spent a decade of his life in the mission field. I hoped to glean as much advice from him as possible. He told me about his days on the mission field and then asked me about my trip. I began to recount some of the difficulties that I had been experiencing recently. Very quickly, he interjected and said that I would not be doing any medical work on this trip. The best that I could hope to accomplish on this trip would be to learn what I could do on future trips. He went on to elaborate that without the proper team it would be virtually impossible to conduct a medical mission. Needless to say, I felt terribly disheartened. His words only confirmed what I felt inside.

As I pondered my predicament, I felt an overwhelming compulsion to tell this gentleman about Loren. I told him about how we met, and then I told him that Loren was leading a medical mission team to Uganda on the exact same week that my trip was planned. In one sentence, this missionary changed the course of my future. He looked at me and said, "It appears that God has opened another door for you." After a few phone calls, our itinerary had completely changed. I felt like a huge weight had been lifted off my shoulders. I had a new team. There were twenty in all. Among the group, there was another doctor who was a full time medical missionary, three nurses, two pharmacists, and an EMT. Even better, I didn't have to do any planning. I simply had to show up. I went with an organization called Helping Hands Foreign Missions, and they took care of all of the details. Once again, God had provided for my every need.

...A Sad Ending...

While we were in Uganda, Denese successfully completed the first part of her rehab. From the reports that we received, she was doing well. Unfortunately, the funding for her rehab ran out sooner than expected, so she didn't get to stay as long as we had hoped. Loren graciously brought Denese back to his home. She stayed with him for several months. The changes that occurred during this time were dramatic. She looked like a new woman. There was a sparkle in her eyes that I hadn't seen before. By all accounts, she was doing better than expected, so our hopes for her continued to remain high.

Against our wishes, Denese continued to cling to a small part of the bridge. We wanted her to cut all ties with it, but she was unable to do so. She was in love with a man named Robert who lived under the bridge. They had been together for years. This relationship would ultimately lead to her undoing. Whenever the opportunity arose, she would visit him at the bridge. She might spend an hour or so with him every week. She refrained from drinking, but I knew that she would relapse if she kept putting herself in this situation. The temptation was just too great.

Sadly, one afternoon, she did succumb to this temptation. She took a drink, and with it, all that she had accomplished in the last few months was washed away. Everything that she had worked for was gone.

It was heartbreaking to watch. I often wondered if there was more that I could have done to save her. Part of me says yes. Another part says no. I could have done any number of things differently, but the decision was ultimately hers to make. This would turn out to be her last chance. She would never leave the bridge again. She kept drinking, and her health kept deteriorating. This went on for a few more months. Then one morning, a police officer arrived at my door to inform me that she had passed away during the night. We knew that this outcome was inevitable. I had tried to prepare myself, but when it happened, I was still crushed. After she died, I began to slowly sink into a state of depression.

Like the story that began this book, it seemed like the rains had come, and I was about to be washed away with it. Denese was gone. My world was falling apart. The story that I had been writing was over. I couldn't see through the downpour that was falling all around me. There was no rainbow or silver lining in the raincloud as far as I could tell. But then God did what only God can do. He took pain and suffering and turned it into something beautiful. He used Denese's death and the anguish that it had created in my life to create a miracle.

...A Miracle...

After returning from Uganda, I went before my church to share with them my experiences from the mission trip. I also used this occasion to introduce them to the Helping Hands organization. I wanted them to hear about the amazing work that they were doing in Uganda. They were in the process of buying land to build "The Village of Eden." It would be a fully functional orphanage. Due to the AIDS epidemic and civil unrest, orphans abounded in the country. Their plan was to use women who were widowed, and thus looked down upon, to care for the orphans. It would be a winning proposition for both. Within the confines of the orphanage, there would be a school, church, medical clinic, and land for farming and tending livestock. This was the future of Helping Hands, and they were raising funds to pursue it.

A couple of months after Denese's death, my pastor pulled me aside and told me about an idea that he had. He called it "Advent Conspiracy." Over the Christmas holiday, he planned on asking the congregation to buy less and give more. More specifically, he wanted to use the Christmas Eve offering to help build a school at the Village of Eden. When the time came, he asked the members of our church to spend a little less on gifts and to donate the difference. He had managed to get another church in the community to join the fundraising campaign. On Christmas Eve, a collection was taken. The services were all well attended. By the end, a stack of checks and dollar bills filled the offering plate. Once it was counted, an amount of $105,000 had been collected. This money was donated to Helping Hands, and the following year the school was built.

I will never forget the moment when I received this news. It was during one of our church services. I was sitting in the pews when I was suddenly hit with the revelation that all of this had been made possible because of Denese. The following sequences of events passed through my mind. I had met Loren because of Denese's willingness to go back to rehab. If she had refused, then we would have never met. The conversation about our mission trips would have never occurred. I would have probably not gone to Uganda and definitely not with Helping Hands. I would have never shared Helping Hand's vision with my church. There probably would not have been an Advent Conspiracy, and even if there had been, the funds would have been channeled elsewhere. Loren was in attendance for the ceremony. After it was over, he walked over to me and said, "This happened because of Denese." I had not uttered a word to him about this. In a rather profound manner, we had experienced the same revelation. At this point, I knew that God had indeed performed a miracle in the most unlikely of ways.

...The Widow's Mite...

Shortly thereafter, I shared this miracle with folks under the bridge during one of the services. I tied it into the message for the day. I wanted to share part of it with you. For the scripture, I chose Luke 21:1-4. It is the story of "The Widow's offering." It reads as follows:

"Jesus looked up and saw the rich putting their gifts into the offering box, and he saw a poor widow put in two small copper coins. And he said, 'Truly, I tell you, this poor widow has put in more than all of them. For they all contributed out of their abundance, but she out of her poverty put in all she had to live on'" (ESV).

In this story, we meet a very unlikely recipient of the Lord's affection, a poor widow. This woman had almost nothing to give. Even for the standards of her own day, she was seemingly insignificant. Yet, we are still reading about her two thousand years later. Her story is one that has been etched into the pages of history. It is a story that has inspired many over the years and been the subject of countless sermons. I wonder if she had any idea how great an impact her actions would make on the world.

She opened her hand, and two little copper coins fell from it. They tumbled and turned, moving in slow motion through the air. Then they clanked and bounced, coming to rest on other coins much more valuable than themselves. From the surface, it seemed rather uneventful, a simple act with seemingly no real significance. But at that very moment, there was an earthquake of epic proportions erupting in the spiritual realm. A tremor began spreading throughout the heavens and onto earth, and we are still feeling the effects of it today.

As I shared the widow's story, I shared Denese's story with them. I felt that there were many similarities. For starters, Denese was extremely poor. In fact, she didn't even have a penny to give. For the most part, I believe that she regretted how her life turned out. I know that she wanted more. But the pain that the world inflicted on her proved too great for her to overcome. However, there was a time in her life, albeit short, when she chose God over her addiction. In this moment, she too gave something seemingly insignificant that God used to change the world.

In the widow's story, she gave something seemingly insignificant. She gave two very small copper coins. It wasn't very much. At the time, it was only worth about a day's wage. It was all that she had, and instead of keeping it for herself, she gave it away. If you analyze her story more closely, you will quickly realize that the widow gave much more than two small coins. She gave all that she had to live on. She had no money left for food, clothing, medicines, or housing. By giving it all away, she was giving up her ability to care for herself. In doing so, she was basically saying, "God, whether you want me or not I am yours. If I live or die, I am yours. I can't take care of myself. I am in your hands now. Do with me as you please." The widow surrendered herself to God. She gave it all. This is why Jesus said, *"Truly, I say to you, this poor widow has put in more than all [those who are contributing to the offering box]"* (ESV). They gave out of their excess. She gave out of her poverty. Jesus knew how much she gave away. Nothing passes by his eyes unnoticed. He knows the total sum of what a person can give, and the most valuable thing that a person can give by far is himself or herself. When the widow dropped those two coins into the offering, she was really offering herself to God.

In February of 2011, Denese was faced with a difficult decision. After years of living her way, she had a choice to make. Her health was deteriorating. To continue in her current lifestyle meant sure death. For years, she had been running from God. She had been hiding within her addiction, but her time was running out. She needed to say "no" to her addiction and finally say "yes" to God. She wasn't sure that she was ready to give up her addiction, lifestyle, friends, and home. Even though continuing in this lifestyle meant sure death, she still found comfort in them. Leaving these things meant that she would have to sober up and face the world, recognize her wrongs, and have a time of reckoning with God. God wanted her to submit to him, but she wasn't ready to completely give herself away. She had a choice to make: alcohol or God. I am proud to say that for a time she chose God. She said "no" to her addiction and "yes" to God. She let go of her bottle and dropped it into the offering. She gave up the very thing that gave her the most comfort. She had been drinking for most of her life. Without it, she was naked, helpless, lost. Yet, she let go of it, and like the widow. I imagine that she said, "God, whether you want me or not I am yours. If I live or die, I am yours. I can't take care of myself. I am in your hands now. Do with me as you please." On that day she walked away from the bridge, leaving the life and home that she had known for so long to offer herself to God.

The widow's actions were seemingly insignificant, yet we find them recorded in the greatest book ever written. Her story has been read and cherished by an untold number. God greatly blessed the widow for her self-sacrifice. To me, his blessing seemed out of proportion, but this is the beauty of God. He can take a small sacrifice and turn it into something monumental. But there is an interesting footnote to the story. I doubt that widow ever realized the significance of her actions. I suspect that she dropped her coins into the offering and then walked away, not realizing that she had just become the center of Jesus' conversation. It probably wasn't until she reached heaven that she realized what a huge impact that she had made on the world. Such was the case for Denese. She died before realizing the difference that she had made. There is no denying the fact that God blessed Denese for her self-sacrifice. Much like the widow, Denese's actions were used by God to change the world. God could have accomplished this feat in any number of ways, but he chose to use Denese because of her willingness to put a sacrificial offering in the plate.

The donations from the Advent Conspiracy campaign were used to build classrooms in Uganda. In an amazing fashion, God used Denese's life to touch others halfway across the world. Generations of orphans will benefit from these classrooms. They will have an opportunity to get a good education, and hopefully, advance to become more than they would have otherwise. Without Denese, there would have been no story to tell my church. There would have been no fund-raiser. There would have been no classrooms. If Denese had not given herself to God, none of this would have occurred, but because she did, God blessed her in a way that she could have never fathomed. Denese didn't have much to give. She didn't have any money. But, she gave away all that she had, and that was herself. For most, this would not be valued as much. She was an addicted, homeless woman living under a bridge. Very few would see any worth in her, but very few saw any worth in an old widow living in ancient Israel either. But God saw great worth in both, and he turned their seemingly insignificant investment into something that would change the world for all of eternity.

Every now and then, I get the opportunity to share this story with someone, and each time, the response is always the same. They are amazed, and for the record, they should be. This was no random sequence of events. God performed a miracle. He planned every detail and then orchestrated it flawlessly despite having to use two very flawed participants, namely myself and Denese. But then again, this is just what he does. He has always been in the business of creating, with miracles being his specialty. I hope that this story has touched you and been a heartfelt reminder that when all seems lost, don't forget to put your faith in God, because the next miracle may be just around the corner.

...The Samaritan Woman

For the conclusion, I am going to finish with a message that I shared at our first social gathering for The Bridge Ministry. When I began this journey, God gave me a piece of scripture that I have subsequently held close to my heart. It is a story that I have read countless times, but on this one occasion, God gave me an entirely new perspective of it. In the ministry's darkest moments, it continued to bring me great hope. It is the story of Jesus and the Samaritan woman found in the book of John chapter 4.

After the invasion of Israel's Northern Kingdom by the Assyrians in the seventh century B.C., Samaria was settled by the Assyrian invaders along with any Jew who had not been taken away into captivity. Intermarrying resulted between the two groups, and their children, the Samaritans, became half-breeds so to speak, being part Jew and Assyrian. This was an abomination to the Jewish people because their culture forbade the marrying of people from other lands. This rule had been created to prevent other cultures from influencing their own. The Samaritans quickly fell into the trap of worshiping the gods of the Assyrians, which was a direct violation of Jewish law. For these reasons, Jews during the time of Jesus did not associate with Samaritans. They despised and looked down on them as if they were an inferior people.

Geographically, Samaria was situated in the middle of the country of Israel. The shortest path between the northern and southern parts of the kingdom was directly through it. However, to avoid passing through Samaria, most Jews chose a path around it. As a result, Samaria had become a forgotten land. In the story of the Samaritan woman, we find Jesus going against the grain once again. Rather than going around Samaria, he has gone into it and taken the twelve disciples with him.

During the trip, Jesus met a woman at a well. It was noontime, the hottest part of the day. It was a time when no other women would be out drawing water. There was a good reason why this woman was out during this time of day. She was an outcast in her community. To avoid meeting others, she went and drew water from the well at a time when no one else would be there. This woman was literally an outcast among outcasts. She was the lowest of the low. She was heading nowhere fast. But, after a short conversation with Jesus, the trajectory of her downward spiral changed one hundred and eighty degrees. I am always amazed by what a single encounter with God can do.

But this wasn't the only miracle in the story. After Jesus saved this poor woman's soul, he used her testimony to start a revival in her hometown. Over the next couple of days, the scripture says that a great many came to be followers of Christ because of the woman's testimony. Jesus started a revival in the most unlikely way. He used a woman who was an outcast among her own people to start a revival. This town was situated right in the middle of Samaria. I can only imagine that this revival had a ripple effect throughout the surrounding countryside, spilling from Samaria into Israel.

Like Samaria, the bridge had also become a forgotten land. The people who lived there were outcasts in their own community. Even among the poor, they were considered outcasts. They were the lowest of the low. On a daily basis, people passed over and around them. For me, the similarities between ancient Samaria and the bridge were quite striking. I have had to caution myself about taking the Samaritan woman's story too literally, but in the back of my mind, I have always wondered if God might use one of the men or women who lived there to start a revival in my community.

From the very beginning, I had always believed that our Samaritan woman would be Denese. I will be the first to admit that her storyline diverges from the one in the Bible. Yet, I still believe that the outcome has the potential to be the same. The prophet Isaiah once wrote, *"As the heavens are higher than the earth, so are my ways higher than your ways and my thoughts than your thoughts"* (Isaiah 55:9 ESV). God is not bound by our limitations. He could recreate this story in any number of ways. For instance, even though Denese has passed away, her words are still alive, echoing throughout the pages of this book. Whether God uses this story for a grander purpose, I do not know. But I will say that God has always shown the unique ability to glorify himself in death. My hope is that he will use this opportunity to stir something within your heart and possibly your community for his purposes. But only time will tell if this dream will ever come to fruition. It is my hope that it will.

AN ALTERNATE ENDING...

AN ALTERNATE ENDING...

Part 1 continued...A Poem...

As Brad was lying over Denese's cold and wet chest,
large tears in his eyes began to coalesce.
With his head still firmly pressed against her chest,
he began pounding his right hand against
Denese's breast.
Then he began to fight and to plead asking,
"Denese, why didn't you listen to me?
This shouldn't have occurred.
If you would have only left the bridge,
your life would still be preserved.
But you didn't want to change your ways,
and this is what resulted.
You allowed fear to dictate your life
and look where it has led.
Instead of being alive and well, you are simply dead.
From your place, you couldn't see
that there was another way to be.
If you would have used your ears for listening,
I could have shown you a life that isn't worth missing.
Amid my own struggles and pains,
I found something worth heavenly gain.

It was during this searching when God I found,
or maybe it was the other way around.
Regardless of who found whom, I know this much to be true.
I know that I will never be the same.
In fact, everything has changed, even my name.

* * *

Now, I call myself Christian,
but the title of Christian is so much more than just a name.
It's a hope in a God who loves nothing more than to
heal the lame.
Oh, how I wish that you had the chance to meet.
With him on your side, there are no odds that you
couldn't have beat.
I am quite certain that your life would have changed.
Yes, it is true that some parts would have needed
to be rearranged.
I firmly believe that if you had found God someway
that instead of being dead that you would be alive today.
But your life ended much too soon,
and with your death, my dreams for you never got to bloom.
Now, all my hopes have been lost,
for they were killed by an early and unwanted frost.

* * *

But wait…could it be?
Is there still a chance for you and me?
An idea just entered my mind;
one that I never expected to find.
I'll grant you this fact. It's an idea that is altogether absurd;
the likes of which I have never heard.
Honestly I don't care.
I will utter that prayer.

God, my voice I don't know if you can hear,
but if you can, please lend me your ear.
My friend here has just passed.
She was a girl with whom I had hoped to build
a relationship that might last.
You see, through her, I discovered something hidden
deep inside of me.
It was a feeling that I didn't know existed,
but the longer I stayed near her the more it persisted,
and over time, this feeling
began to change the very fiber of my being.
This feeling of which I speak is love.
Because of Denese,
my heart has learned to soar high above.
And through my love,
I hoped that hers would do the same,
but now my Denese is gone,
and I fear that my love for her won't live on.
If it wouldn't be too much to ask,
I was wondering if you might break death's trance
and give my friend, Denese, a second chance."

* * *

Upon uttering this simple prayer,
something strange began to fill the air.
In that moment, the rains halted,
and then the clouds parted.
And this occurrence was followed by a most glorious sight,
For the Son had come down to help Brad with his plight.
Like a white dove,
he descended from heaven above.
Through the air, he appeared to float,
and ultimately, he came to rest on the water without a boat.

But he didn't sink as one might think.
No, he floated just the same, and a water walker he became.
Over to Brad's position, the Son did tread,
and by this point, Brad's heart had been filled
with a great deal of dread.
But the Son sensed the trepidation growing within Brad's head.
He said, "Do not fear.
I have only noble reasons for being here.
You called with a most sincere request,
and to your plea, I have chosen to acquiesce."

* * *

"Sir, may I ask a simple question of you.
I know not who you are or what you intend to do."

* * *

"Well, the truth is that I have many different names, but alto-
gether, their purposes have always been the same.
From the beginning, I have been called the Lamb.
The one known as the great I AM,
because as you will soon see,
I can be whatever it is that I need to be.
For purpose of today,
the aspect of healer is what I will display.
Before I proceed, there is something that I must say.
I have seen your struggles and felt your pain.
I know through Denese what you had hoped to gain.
At the present, you believe that your struggles
were all for naught,
but this is simply not true because much you have been taught.
Oh, Brad, my precious child, can't you see
that it was because of her that you ultimately found me?
Now, the reverse will soon be true

because Denese is going to find me through you.
Still yet, there is something that you don't know.
The truth is that both of you had died long ago.
But through me, your soul is no longer dead,
for it has been resurrected.

* * *

Now, for Denese, I must do the same,
and once done, she too will have a new name.
For you will become my children, one and the same.
And this family to which I speak has Christian for its name.
This family, I command you to love and to cherish.
And I implore you to invite others in
so that they won't perish.
Without a doubt, you have to be bold
because your story is one that needs to be told.
Proclaim it to all who will listen
but don't be discouraged when they sneer and hiss
for the point of it all many will miss.
Through you, some will find the way,
and for both that will be a glorious day.
With that said, it is time for your miracle to continue,
the one which was born at the very first bridge venue.
Dear Denese, it is time for you to awake.
So arise dear sleeper and come up from the lake!

* * *

To this command, Denese's body was revived,
and Brad was truly shocked to see her alive.
Around Denese's neck, his arms he placed,
and then he scattered kisses all over her face.
Brad turned to thank the Son,
but during that time, the Son had gone.

The vestige of his image was nowhere to be found;
not in the sky nor on the ground.
Above, the sun no longer shone
because the clouds had once again grown.
But in his heart, a light had been lit,
and no amount of rain could ever drown it.
Turning to Denese, Brad told her his tale,
and once he had finished, the truth did prevail.

* * *

From there, the two journeyed into the town
that had become very run down.
You see Happyville was no longer happy;
in fact, it had become altogether unhappy.
The years of striving in vain
had left it in a great deal of pain.
In the town, the tale they boldly told,
and it penetrated hearts that had long since grown cold.
People received their message with much gladness,
for they found that it had the power to wash away
all of their sadness.
A revival of sorts did ensue,
the likes of which they never knew.
From youngest of young to the oldest of old,
people of all ages began to come into the fold.
From Happyville, the word did spread,
and many found that they were no longer dead.
And finally to the bridge, many people came
with a purpose that was exactly the same.
They rebuilt that old bridge, plank by plank,
and then they carried Denese home so her father
they could thank.
For without Denese, this story would have not occurred,

and the events which just happened would have
never been stirred.

* * *

But as it was the rain had begun to stop,
and from the sky, the clouds had begun to drop.
And when the sky had become nice and clear,
the people saw something on the frontier.
It was something that they had never before seen,
and in the sunlight, they couldn't help but be
drawn to its gleam.
For up on the ridge,
they saw a most magnificent bridge.
And upon the bridge a beautiful sight had begun to crest,
for it was there that a brilliant rainbow had come to rest.

All the proceeds from this book will be donated to
Helping Hands Foreign Missions
in honor of Denese for the continuation of
The Village of Eden project.

If you wish to donate to this cause,
please visit their website at
www.helpinghandsmissions.org
or mail to
Helping Hands Foreign Missions
5043 Bristol Industrial Way
Buford, GA 30518

ABOUT THE AUTHOR

Brad Pierce is a board certified physician in Internal Medicine. He received his B.S. degree from the University of Georgia before attending to the Medical College of Georgia. He completed his residency at Wake Forest University. He moved to Gainesville, Georgia in 2004 where he has practiced medicine for the last ten years. He is married to Meredith Pierce and has two children, Hunter and Halle. Brad is active in his local church, The Bridge Ministry, and foreign missions. His life mission is helping others connect to God in a deeper and more intimate way.

ACKNOWLEDGMENTS

I am grateful to Meredith Pierce, Bill Edmonds, Brennan Wood, Jim Armstrong, and Sean Allen for their valuable contributions to this book.